Sweet Temptations:

Ménage à Trois

L.M. Mountford

Edited by readabit: Copy Editing and Proofreading Services Est 2018

L.M. Mountford – 1st Ed.
ISBN: 978-1-913945-96-1

THE LORD OF LUST PUBLICATIONS

Sweet Temptations:

MÉNAGE À TROIS

L.M. MOUNTFORD

The author highly recommends your read books one and two of the Sweet Temptations Trilogy before reading this concluding instalment.

If you haven't read them already, Book One can be downloaded for FREE here:

Chapter One

Alice Martin wasn't a woman to beat about the bush.

She knew what she wanted and when she saw it, she went for it.

It had been that way the night she first met her husband. It hadn't mattered that he was at work or that they hadn't formally met, or didn't even know each other's names. She'd seen him, she'd wanted him, so she took him.

If she wanted something, the technicalities just didn't matter.

So when she saw a particular garment hanging in the window of the Bristol high street's

Sweet Temptations Boutique, and felt that all too familiar draw, it had only been a matter of time.

Now fresh from a shower, with her hair still damp and her latest purchase hanging from her shoulders, she couldn't help grinning as she admired her reflection in her vanity.

The cherry red spaghetti strap gown was pure mulberry silk with a black lace trim and clung to her body in all the right ways to emphasise her curves and mile-long legs.

It was perfect. Richard wouldn't know what hit him.

Just the thought of modelling it for him when he came home, of lying stretched out across their bed waiting for him to find her and fuck her brains out, sent a delicious thrill sizzling through her. Beneath the silk, her poor neglected pussy clenched, and her clit, still stiff and begging to be played with, throbbed, reminding her of how close she'd come during that session she'd orchestrated for him during her break.

Damn her and her blasted ideas. This wasn't how it was supposed to be. That call was only supposed to be a warmup *for him*. A tease to get *him* worked up and hard and oh so desperate to take her. Instead, it had backfired and left her feeling restless and on edge. She'd been unable to settle her mind on anything. In short, she was so fucking horny, it was all she could do not to fish out 'Antonio' from her bedside draw and start the party early.

Just the thought of the wand's intense vibrations rumbling against her pussy had her thighs rubbing together in a vain effort to settle the need burning inside her.

It would have felt so good too, but instead she forced herself into action and, taking the matching robe from the hook on the door, she turned and hurried out into the hall. There was too much left to do. She couldn't afford to indulge herself, yet.

Especially when, so far anyway, everything had been going according to plan.

Everything was arranged. She'd left work early to beat Richard home, dropping her last class of the day on a colleague who owed her a favour and missing the ever notorious M5 rush hour. Her parents had said they were fine looking after Alexander for a couple of nights so he was all taken care of, and she had sent everyone else they knew a polite, but firm, text message, warning they weren't to be disturbed.

Tonight was to be theirs.

A quiet candlelit evening just for them, to let go of all their woes, reacquaint themselves with each other's bodies, and give in to all their carnal desires.

It was just what they needed. What they both needed.

Though he said nothing about it, she knew Richard had been feeling stressed. It was all the usual stuff, really, just the little things. Under pressure at his new job. Worried about money. The stresses of moving to a new city and starting a family. Fairly mundane, but her husband had always insisted on dealing with it all by himself, and it was taking a toll on him.

She wanted to help ease his burden, to take them back to how they used to be, even if it was only for one brief night.

And there was always that other thing.

That one little thing a small part of her was so insecure about.

Alice wasn't usually the jealous type, but where Richard was concerned, she was possessive. She was possessive as hell, and it had not escaped her notice that other women were taking an interest in her husband. Of course, he had always been a good-looking man, but age, it seemed, agreed with him. The cute puppy she'd cornered in the stockroom had grown up into a fox that any red-blooded woman would have to be blind not to notice. And when they did, she had to resist the urge to go up to them and claw their eyes out.

Normally, she had the urge under control. However, Scarlet's undisguised flirtations at the party had been the last straw.

Richard was hers. Her lover. The father of her baby. Her soul mate, and it was time she reaffirmed their bond.

Just imagining all the ways she could have her way with him, could brand him, mark him as hers, had her lip twisting devilishly as she slipped into the kitchen to rummage through the fridge. She could get the ice cream out now, so that it melted a bit first. Or maybe it would be better to start with the wet celery, as they still had the flying helmet from that Halloween party the year before they moved and she could always use the egg whisk on his-

A frantic shriek sounded from somewhere on the floor above.

Chapter Two

What the?

Alice's eyes widen at the sound, so high with pain and fear, like an animal caught in a trap. Forgetting her train of thought, her eyes darted up to the ceiling. It sounded like it had come from the Blaire's flat, but that could have been a trick of the building. The tower block's walls were paper thin and often as not, she could hear several things going on at once from any number of directions that sounded like they were coming from somewhere else. Just the other night she'd been treated to overhearing one couple's marathon sex session that had clearly sounded like it was coming from that very flat upstairs, but couldn't. After all, Richard had been up there after all, helping Rebecca with her computer.

A pity, if he hadn't been upstairs, it would have made quite the mood starter...

Another scream went out, louder this time and much more distinctive.

Rebecca. Alice's heart leapt into her throat.

"You worthless bitch!" a gruff voice half slurred, half barked, followed by the crash of something heavy smashing into glass, shattering it. "Stay still!"

Alice didn't wait for him to get his eye in.

Wheeling on her heel, she made straight for her front door, hurriedly tying the sash of her robe as she went. Another scream, louder, echoing as footsteps ran down the building's stairwell. Then suddenly they were on the landing, running, growing louder by the second as Alice ran to the door.

No sooner had she wrenched it open than Rebecca barrelled into her.

Just managing to catch herself, Alice pulled the girl to her, her arms going around her in a protective hug. "Hey, hey Rebecca, honey, what's happened? What's going on?"

"He's coming, please... I didn't touch... don't let him..." Sobbing, she clung to the older woman, her big doe eyes pleading, so wide they were almost round. The poor thing was terrified out of her mind.

The sight tore at Alice's heart and she pulled her closer, doing her best to sooth her with quiet words. "Shh… honey, it's okay, I won't, nothing's going to happen to you, I promise."

She almost couldn't believe this was the same girl she knew. Rebecca was always so upbeat and bubbly. Of course, she'd known there were some problems in the home. Even a blind man could have seen was nervous around her father and that he could be hard on her, too hard sometimes, but this…

The thought lit a fire in her mother's heart that threatened to burn them both to cinders. That the brute could do this to his own daughter. Drive such a sweet girl to such a fit of terror, sickened her to her very core. What parent, no, what kind of fucking beast could do such a thing?

Struggling to keep her tone soothing, Alice slowly steered Rebecca inside. "Come on, let's get you inside and I'll-"

"Come back here you little bitch!" the other voice bellowed from above amidst a thunder of footsteps. Then he was there on the bend on the stairs, Derik Blaire, red faced with murder and madness scorching his wild eyes. "Where is it, I want it, you fucking whore," he seethed, half lumbering down the last few steps like a hippopotamus, not even seeming to notice Alice. "You hear me? You're a whore. Just a fucking whore, like that bitch mother of yours, now give it to me!"

Rebecca stiffened at her father's call, her knuckles going white like bone as she clung on with a death grip. However Alice hardly noticed as she turned to look at the man. With a gaze as cool as ice, she gently pried herself free. Then, with a gently push, she urged the girl inside the flat. "Go inside," she instructed, her tone firm but just soft enough so that Derik wouldn't overhear. "Lock the door. I'll knock and call for you when it's safe to come out."

"No, please… don't leave me, don't let him-" Rebecca's eyes were glassy with tears and visibly pleaded for Alice not to leave her as she tried to cling to her arm. It was the same look she saw in the eyes of many kids on their first day of school, when their parents left them at the gates for the first time.

"I won't. Go on, I'll take care of this. You go put a brew on." It tore at Alice's heart, but she pushed her inside regardless and pulled the door shut with a firm slam.

She felt like a bitch for it but it was the only way. She couldn't deal with the problem at hand if she was concerned for the girl.

"What the fuck you think you're doing, bitch? Get the fuck out of my way!" he slurred angrily, staggering to a stop only a metre or so from Alice, swaying from one foot to the other. As if only just seeing her for the first time, he grinned in a way that made her feel dirty just for him looking at her.

"Alright *John*, I don't know what you're on tonight, but I think you need to go back upstairs and sleep it off." Alice wouldn't be cowed. He may have towered over her, but she was well accustomed to dealing with people bigger than her. She held his gaze with steely determination, doing her best to ignore the fact that the only thing protecting her modesty was a silk robe that showed off way too much leg and did nothing to hid the swell of her bosom.

"Don't you tell me what to do, you little cow," he slurred, sneering down at her. "I've had it with all you posh tossers... talking down to me... treating me like shit... That whore in there... took my shit... and now she's going to give it back or I'm gonna beat her ass black and blue then throw it out on the street." The thick stink of booze was coming off him in waves. He'd definitely had more than a skinful.

"No," Alice said firmly. "You're not going anywhere near her in that state. So just go back upstairs before I-"

"You'll what?" Derik Blaire barked, his mouth spreading into a mocking grin that could have curdled milk as he stepped forward, closing the gap. "What are you gonna do? Don't give me all that shit... Your man's not here to protect you. What you going to do to me, you little bitch? How are you going to stop me from taking whatever I want from your fat arse..." The threats were almost as ugly as he was. With that squat face crowned by a brush of chestnut-grey hair and a body like a barrel that had been sat on by something heavy one too many times, he gave the faint impression of being the love child of Bruce Willis and Ray Winstone. Only without the charisma, good looks, or height.

He was taller than her though. And that must have made him feel cocky because he loomed over her. Enough that she knew he'd be able to see straight down the valley of her cleavage soon enough. One of his hands slowly reached out to touch.

"You know, I'm sick and tired of you and limp dick treating me like I'm shit. Don't know why a cunt like you puts up with him. Look at those fat tits and ass… come on bitch, let me have a feel… mmm… too good for him… maybe it's time I show you how a real man treats his bitc-"

His words died with a sickening wet crunch.

Just before his fingers could touch the slope of her right breast, Alice rammed the heel of her palm up into his nose. Blood arced, and he wheeled away, howling in agony.

"Don't touch me," she growled. The very idea of this *thing* laying a hand on her provoked a fresh surge of fiery rage inside her. How fucking dare he, this… *beast* think he could touch her, even lay a single, filthy fucking finger on her.

Derik Blaire gave no sign of having heard her, however.

"Bitch… you broke my nose," he spat out, glaring at her with both hands clamped up to the ruin of his nose. Blood was oozing out from between his fingers.

"Yeah, I did," Alice shot back, and slowly she sunk down into the ready stance her instructors had ingrained into her, ready to spring to the attack. It felt awkward to assume the position again, but once upon a time, the position had been as natural to her as any. "Try to touch me again, and next time I'll break your hand and shove it so far down your throat, you'll be scratching your balls."

His eyes widened, perhaps surprised by her threat, then narrowed dangerously as hate and anger burned through whatever was left of his common sense.

"Scratch this." He lunged, cranking his fist back and swinging it up and around. It was a decent effort. If it landed, it might very well have taken her head off, but he was nowhere near fast enough. Pissed as a skunk as he was, the attack was pitifully obvious and Alice danced away, ducking down under his arm then sidestepping as his momentum carried him by. Whatever it lacked in subtlety, the robe made up for in freedom of movement, if nothing else.

Derik wheeled around after her, faster than anyone could have expected from a man so deep in his cups, bellowing his fury like a barbarian. His second swing was smaller, but the distance between them was so slight, she couldn't dodge him this time. Nor had she meant to. Instead, she closed the gap. Stepping in and driving her left forearm up into the hook of his arm, stopping it dead, as she folded her right arm and swung it up, clubbing his broken nose with her elbow.

The sudden explosion of pain obviously seared across the man's brain as his head jarred back and as his knees gave way. He went down hard, collapsing on his back to lie in a heap, conscious but dazed and soon to be in a lot of pain.

Alice turned away, walked back to her flat door, raised a hand to knock, and the door open. Rebecca stood behind it, her eyes wide but her look of terror now replaced by a mix of puzzlement and disbelief. Clearly, she had been watching everything through the peephole.

"How…" she started but seemed to think better of it halfway through and instead went with. "I mean, he was, and you're so- I mean a…"

"My dad was in the SAS," Alice said, like that should have explained it all, stepping inside and shutting the door on the sight of Derik Blaire lying there on the landing, broken and bruised, like some beached walrus. "When the boys at school started teasing me, he had the PT instructors give me some private coaching, then had me doing drills with the lads at *The Lines* over the weekends. They even let me run the selection march across the Brecon Beacons over summer holidays, and no boy ever pulled my pigtails again."

That wasn't strictly true. There had been a few who had tried to make fun of 'the little girl', but they hadn't been laughing for long. A throat punch could be one hell of a punch line, especially when delivered by a girl half your size.

The memory made Alice's mouth curl, then she took in the sight of Rebecca's pale and haggard face and it fell away. "Come on, honey, let's go get you cleaned up."

Chapter Three

Richard's phone was dead when Alice tried to call him, probably because he'd been called into a last-minute meeting. Probably that bitch, Scarlet, trying to get her revenge. If so, there was no telling how long it would go on for, so she just fired off a quick text, explaining what had happened, in the briefest possible terms.

There was no need to go into details, no point worrying him.

Once the tick appeared alongside the message on the screen, showing the text had been delivered, she put it down on the side. With no further use for the device, she picked up her freshly brewed mug of tea and headed to the bathroom.

She walked in without knocking.

Inside, the air was hot and humid. The windows were fogged and condensation rolled down the tiled walls in rivulets as Rebecca sat in a bath of hot water, hugging her knees to her chest. She didn't look up as Alice sat down on the side of the tub, but she had got a little colour back.

Alice offered her the mug. "Here you go, honey. Have a sip of this,".

Rebecca, however, just kept her head down and stared blankly into nothingness. Or perhaps she was just too fascinated by the last few soap suds floating across the water's surface to notice.

Alice carried on regardless.

"Not thirsty?" She set the cup down on the floor, then softly started stroking the girl's thick waves of dark chocolate hair. "That's okay. Take as long as you need. You're safe, I promise…"

She had such beautiful hair, so thick and silky smooth. She should stop wearing it in that silly side braid. It suited her down, in a beautiful unbound wash that would probably go all the way down to her butt. And what a butt it wa-

No, stop it! Alice chastised herself. There was a time and a place for such thoughts, and this sure as hell wasn't the time. Though she could have thought of worse places than a hot bath and with that in mind, she decided there were better ways to comfort the lass, as well as keep her hands busy.

Rebecca instinctively stiffened as the older woman pulled her into a hug, but Alice did not pull back. Instead, she tried to draw her against her even tighter, rocking softly from side to side, desperate to give the girl all the feelings of closeness and security she knew she needed.

She softened slightly after a moment, then completely as inside, the walls began to crumble.

When she finally spoke, her voice was a whisper. "Really?"

Alice's heart soared, yet she kept her voice even and neutral to not spook the girl. "Really what, honey?"

"Safe?" Her voice was a little stronger with that one syllable, the hope behind it almost tangible, but there was a tremble there too, as if she hung on a knife's edge, about to fall through the ice at any moment. "You said I'm safe... did you mean it? Really?"

The desperate hope in that one question raked Alice and she could feel the tears burning at the corners of her eyes. God, what had that monster done to her? "Yes, of course I did, honey," she promised, "I promise. You'll always be safe with us."

The words sounded hollow to her own ears and woefully inadequate, but Rebecca must have heard the sincerity in them because, slowly, she tilted her head up. Her big doe eyes glistening as they met the older woman's. "Thank you."

It was all she could muster before the last of her walls came down. Her tears flowed freely as she threw her arms around the older woman and buried her head into the crook of Alice's neck, shaking with the sobs. Alice hugged her through it, doing her best to comfort her even as her face grew wet with her own silent sobs for the girl's plight.

"It's okay, I promise, it's all going to be alright," she soothed, lying as much as hoping, not really knowing what else to say. How could anything ever be alright again? Domestic abuse was an ugly thing, destroying even more lives than it took, and the effects could haunt the victims for years after. How was she ever going to live a 'normal' life?

Alice didn't have any answers, so she did her best to just comfort the girl as all her grief and fear came pouring out of her. Then, as quickly as it had hit, the storm passed.

"I'm sorry, oh god, acting like that, I'm so embarrassed…" Rebecca said when the tears ceased, her reddening eyes downcast and uncertain as she pulled away and slid back into the bathwater. Full as it was, the soapy water came up to the tops of her breasts.

"Honey, it's okay," Alice said gently, retrieving the mug from the floor and handing it to her. "Do you want to talk about it?"

Rebecca didn't respond. The question hung in the air between them. Alice waited patently. She didn't want to push Rebecca too far, but she also wanted to give her the chance to speak before the memories took root inside her, like a rot.

Slowly, Rebecca took a long swig of the tea, stealing herself. It would have been half cold, but it was better than nothing.

"*He* thought I'd stolen something." Rebecca spoke softly, but the venom with which she spat the word emphasised it more than if she had screamed it out. "Turns out he'd known all along I was saving up to move out. So, when he couldn't find something on his desk, he realised I'd had someone round…" Alice felt a lump forming in her throat, remembering how she had half encouraged Richard to go help the girl. "I told him I didn't know anything about it, but he didn't believe me, just started shouting things. He'd already had a lot to drink by the time I got home. Normally he stops after he's screamed himself out a bit, but this time he just kept getting worse, then when he started throwing things, I just panicked and ran."

"Oh, honey…" There were so many other things Alice wanted to say, to tell her, to reassure her things could get better, but when Rebecca began sobbing again, they all caught in her throat. Instead, she just pulled her back into another close hug.

Rebecca carried on regardless, the words pouring out of her in the rush of fresh emotion. "He never used to be like this. When I was little, he was always so kind and would play with me and take me out for drives or trips to the park, and then the pool or the cinema. But after mum left… oh god, what am I going to do now? I can't go back home, but all my stuff is up there, and I haven't got nearly enough saved to find a place of my own yet… so I… but how can I…"

Alice didn't have an answer. She didn't have any answers. How could she? The girl's world had just been turned upside down and inside out, then given her a prompt kick in the teeth for her trouble. It fucking sucked, but answers for things so large took time to be worked out. So, once again, she just held her, hugged her close, and let her get everything out. All the while enjoying the feeling of the girl's warm body pressed so close against her own through the robe.

She was sure Richard had thought she was joking, or just playing a game when she'd remarked on how beautiful the girl was. He wasn't completely wrong, but she wouldn't deny either that she had more than once admired the girl's long legs in those tight little jeans she always wore and wondered what it would feel like to have them wrapped around her head as she feasted on her sweet little pussy.

Such fantasies were her naughty little secret, and she'd never been ashamed of them, but she wasn't about to let them ruin her marriage either. It wasn't that she was in the closet, or that she'd ever officially claimed to be bisexual, but then, she'd never said she was straight, ether. Straight, Bi, Gay, they were all labels, and Alice hated labels. Why should she define herself, or for that matter, what made other people think they could brand her like a cow on the block?

She was just her. Alice Martin. Mother, wife and teacher, that was all and in that order. Everything else was no one else's business.

Then again, she'd never told him that when they'd first hooked up, she'd been involved in an unofficial, on again off again fling with her roommate Samantha. Nor that it had continued after they'd started going steady, and that it had only stopped when they'd got married. Even then, while they had both moved on and settled down into actual relationships, occasionally, whenever she or Sam had felt the itch, they would arrange a girl's night to relive old times.

Richard had never asked much about the nights, so she'd never lied to him about it.

It was foolish and reckless, she knew, and after, on the drive home, she always promised herself it would be the last. She loved her husband, but there was just something about sex with another woman that she craved as well. She just couldn't help it.

It was so thrilling, feeling the graceful softness of another woman's body on hers, the way they shuddered and writhed in the throes of ecstasy beneath her, and their sweet moans as they soared over the edge…

Not to mention their instinctive skill for knowing just how and when to touch. The old man's adage was very apt and true. Only a woman knew what women wanted…

"You can stay with us," she said without thinking. An idea spurred as much by the heat rising off the bath and the lush floral scent of the girl's hair fogging her thoughts, as the devious ideas haunting her fantasies. "Stay as long as you need."

It was a stupid idea, and Alice could have kicked herself for saying it. The flat was too small, there wasn't room for them all. Where would she stay? There were only two bedrooms, and only one bed… where would she sleep, in bed with her and Richard- *no no… don't go there, don't go there.*

But it was too late. Her mind was already swimming with thoughts and ideas…

Naughty, dirty thoughts and ideas that sent a tingle of delicious shivers straight down to her core, making her pussy slick and clit throb once more.

"What?" Rebecca gasped, stilling for a moment, her eyes going wide as she looked up slowly from Alice's shoulder. For the briefest moment, she looked terrified, yet no sooner had their gazes met than she looked down, her lower lip trembling. "Oh, um… thank you, Miss Martin… for everything, you've been so kind, and I… but I can't stay here, I don't deserve it… I… I…"

Her words came out in a rush, and the self-loathing in them set a fire in Alice's soul.

Rising a hand to Rebecca's chin, she tilted the girl's head so she couldn't look away. Her big doe eyes were round and questioning, desperate for comfort and reassurance. "Oh no, no, no… don't say that. You've done nothing wrong." Breathless, Alice could feel her heart racing as she slowly dipped her head down. "None of this is your fault."

Rebecca shook her head, to overcome by the moment to notice. "No, it's not him. I've done something… something horrible. I'm a terrible person and I don't deserve-"

Alice's mouth silenced any further objections.

Chapter Four

It was an accident. She hadn't meant to kiss her, but when the moment came, Alice just couldn't help herself. She crushed her mouth to Rebecca's soft pink lips, all the pent-up lust and desire that had been building up inside her, crashing over the banks and sweeping her away.

Perhaps shocked by the act, Rebecca didn't respond or pull away. Just made an adorable whimper in the back of her throat as Alice's lips slid over hers. Acutely aware of the gorgeous body against hers, so firm and tight but also soft in all the right places, Alice pressed on. Sliding her arms around her waist, she crushed her to her, making

Rebecca gasp before thrusting her tongue into her mouth to feast on the sweetness within.

Deep down, a small voice warned that she should slow down. That she might scare the girl off if she was too forward too fast, but she couldn't help it. She wanted this little minx, wanted her in every way she could have her, and the fire raging down in her centre only drove her on. She kissed her hungrily, needing nothing else in that moment so much as to possess her, consume her, devour her completely. Her tongue curling round and round in the soft little brushes and slides that always made Alice's knees weak, until all the tension flowed from her young conquest in a low purring moan.

Then she was kissing her back, sucking on her tongue with a greedy hunger, those soft lips working up and down like she was sucking a cock. The very idea of it made Alice's skin tingle and pussy throb, and she couldn't help her own little moan when Rebecca grabbed her. One hand fisting her hair while the other clawed at her ass through the silk, almost dragging her into the tub. It was a deliciously aggressive act that she would never have guessed would explode from her doe-eyed babysitter, and one that pushed all her hot buttons. She knew what she wanted, and with girls she always enjoyed being the top, but it wasn't fun unless they played too…

Not to be outdone, however, she reciprocated, pulling the girl up and out of the bath. Water ran off her in a shower of rivulets and miniature waterfalls, splashing across the floor, but Alice hardly noticed or cared. She turned and backed her up against the bathroom wall, pushing one thigh between those long legs, pinning her there.

Rebecca gasped at the unexpected contact, her back curling in sweet surprise. Greedily swallowing the sounds, Alice slowly rocked and ground her thigh against the girl's bare pussy, delighting in the feeling of her slick heat. When she couldn't take it anymore, Rebecca broke away, a long sultry moan pouring from the circle of her lips as the friction drove her wild.

"Mmm… I love the way you taste… so sweet and naughty… so sexy…" Alice purred, leaning up to tease Rebecca's ear with her tongue as Rebecca's hips continued circling against her thigh. Her pussy was drenched. "Mmmm… I can't wait to eat your pretty little pussy."

"Oh god… Mrs… Mrs Martin… wait… We shouldn't…" With her breathing ragged, the girl couldn't get the words out but rolled her head back, offering more skin.

"No, I want you." Dipping her head, Alice attacked the graceful slope of her throat with hot, fiery nips before soothing the tender flesh with her tongue. "I want you to cum for me. Right here. Right now."

"But what about… Mr Martin…" Rebecca got out, all the while trying to drag her ravisher closer. Her nails bit into her skin through her robe as she answered each grind with one of her own in a desperate plea for more. Her question fell off into another wanton moan when Alice sucked her pulse spot.

She wanted it. Alice knew it. She could see it written in her eyes, dark with lust. Had felt the truth of it in the heat and hunger of her kiss. Yes, she wanted this, but there was something else, something holding her back. Fear perhaps. Fear of the consequences, of what it could mean.

It didn't matter. By the time she was done, she'd have forgotten them all.

"I doubt he'd mind," she said, pressing her thigh a little harder against the girl's pussy and the little bundle of nerves hidden within. "Coming home to find his wife eating out their babysitter..." Her own heart was racing with the idea. Just picturing Richard walking in and finding them like this got her so hot, one of her hands came up to cup Rebecca's breast. It felt amazing. So soft but also full and firm and as incredible as she'd imagined, it filled her hand completely. The peaked nipple poked into her palm, begging for attention. "Do you think he'd join us right away, or sit back and watch?"

"Mrs... Martin... Please... I-I...." Alice's clit throbbed with each hitch in Rebecca's voice whenever she rolled her palm over the stiff peak. The sound was so delicious, she wanted nothing more than to fuck a few more out of her.

Reluctantly, Alice abandoned her prize to raise the hand up to Rebecca's check. Cupping her jaw, she gently angled her face so she was looking her in the eye, wanting her to see the truth in her words. "He doesn't know I like girls, too. Won't he be *surprised*. He might want to watch, but I think he'd rather join us. We talked about this just the other morning, after he helped you after you babysat for us."

"You did? But I thought you would be ma-" The girl's eyes widened and there was a tremor in her voice that had nothing to do with the leg pressing against her cleft. A hint of something Alice couldn't bear right now. So she silenced her with a kiss, sealing her mouth over Rebecca's and sliding her tongue in to chase the demons away with slow, luxurious licks.

"It got him so hard, thinking about your perfect tits and this cute little butt..." she growled huskily, sliding her other hand downward. Fingers outstretched and feeling their way along the smooth flesh, teasing along the swells of her buttocks to the lush heat beneath. "Oh, he became a beast, telling me all the things he would do to you... then I suggested sharing you..."

"Please... Mrs Martin... I... we- Oh!" Rebecca buried her face in the crook of the woman's neck, low moans flowing from her thick and sweet as honey. Almost of their own volition, her knees slid apart as the digits brushed along her slick folds.

"That's it, open up for me honey, yes, let me in, good girl... mmm... you're so wet." Sliding one finger through folds into the slick heat, she grinned inwardly at the feeling of Rebecca's walls clenched around her digit, begging for more. "He fucked me so hard and deep, telling me how good this sweet little pussy tasted... how much he loved the feel of it wrapped around his cock, milking out every drop of his cum..." The memory of his cock pummelling her poor pussy with a mad beastly intensity that left her aching and unable to walk straight for most of the day sent a hot shiver tingling through her.

"You... Oh god... You mean you don't... don't mind?" Rebecca's mouth pressed so close to Alice's ear she could feel her desperation shivering through her skin.

It gave her such a sense of conquest. Knowing she'd done this to her. Reduced her to this luscious little wanton. But it wasn't enough. She wanted to take her all the way. To take this little good girl to bed and draw out the sex kitten that lurked beneath the surface.

"Mmm... would you like that, honey? Is that what you want? To feel my husband go balls deep in this tight little pussy and give you the fucking of your life?" she asked, easing her finger out then back in, adding a second finger as she did.

"Oh!" the girl gasped, the feeling of crashing over her and carrying her away. "Yes... please...

please... I... I... oh god, yes, please, I... I... want... it, I want it..."

"Mmmm... your so fucking wet." Alice didn't let up. Sliding her fingers in and out, she felt and teased every part of the slick, delicate tissues she could reach, trying to touch as much of Rebecca as possible. "Are you going to cum? You're going to get this pussy nice and creamy for my husband's cock. Yeah, that's it baby, say it..."

"Oh god, yes! Yes! Please Mrs Martin, I want it, I - oh fuck, oh fuck, fuck, fuck..." She was close. Growing more frantic, she arched up onto tiptoes and curled one long leg over Alice's. Granting her thrusting fingers deeper access as she circled her hips into each plunge.

Fuck, she was so sexy. Alice couldn't wait to have her spread out beneath her in her marital bed, watching her arch and scream and cum over and over as she did such wicked things to her. "Say you want it as I make you cum all over my fingers."

Curling her stroking fingers, she reached out to that spot of roughened flesh beneath her clit. One touch was enough to have Rebecca's back curling as she threw her head back with a shuddered moan of surrender. "Fuck, yes! Please, I want to fuck your husband again, Mrs Martin!"

"Good gir-" Alice froze, her sense of conquest suddenly forgotten as she realised what the girl had just said. "Wait, what?"

However, Rebecca didn't hear the question, or the dangerous lowness to her seducer's voice. Her every focus was on the fingers buried inside her, and the fact they had stopped. Breathing hard and ragged breaths, she shook her head, almost mad with her closeness, mindless with that desperate clawing need to cum. "No! No, please, don't stop, I want his cock again, Mrs Martin, please, please, let me fuck your husband again... please, please, plea-"

"What!"

Chapter Five

Her fury was cold and sharp, cutting through
the spell of the moment like a knife.

"W-hat?" Rebecca blinked, confused, her
voice shaky as she was rudely dragged back from the
brink and thrown into icy reality by the sense of
Alice's fingers leaving her.

Alice just glared at her, her eyes so cold they
almost blazed. Yet, for all her palpable fury, when she
spoke, her voice was even. "What do you mean 'fuck
him again'?"

"You mean you didn't..." she began, shaking
her head, as if not understanding the question. "But...
but you said... he told you and you talked about-"

Alice rolled her eyes. "We role-played my over-hearing him fuck you that night, and-" As she said it, the wheels in her head suddenly turned and a piece fell into place. Realisation dawned, sending a cold wash cascading down her back to leave her legs feeling shaky. Her heart raced, beating a thunderous tempo in her ears. "Oh god, that was you! Wasn't it? Both of you." Her voice flared, going from icy cool to a raging inferno. "He fucked you that night, didn't he?"

Rebecca was shaking, her eyes wet and glassy. "Yes, but Mrs Martin, please I didn't, it just... happened, I never meant... I'm so sorry..." she sobbed, her words a desperate plea. But a plea for what? For her to understand? To forgive? Maybe both, or perhaps something else...

Alice searched the girl's face. Again, that small part of her spoke up. She wanted to believe her. There was no lie in her eyes. That was true. Only fear and worry. They were almost like the eyes of one of her pupils, when she'd caught them doing something they knew was wrong, and awaited the inevitable punishment. But just like those brats, there was no regret. She didn't regret having sex with her husband. In fact, she had probably been planning to do *him* again.

How fucking dare she!

She let out a sigh, jealousy enveloping her like the coils of a monstrous python. "No. No you're not. Not yet."

Rebecca's eyes went wide. She opened her mouth to say something, her pretty little mouth with lips swollen from the kiss, but all that came out was a squeak of surprise as Alice grabbed her arm. In no mood to hear whatever she had to say, she just spun on her heel and dragged her out the door, across the hall, and through the door to the master bedroom. Kicking the door shut behind them, she threw the girl to the bed, where she landed with a bounce. Then she just lay there, unmoving in a dishevelled, beautiful heap upon the bed, with her dark hair spread out beneath her, her eyes downcast, and puffy lips quivering.

The sight stoked the embers still smouldering in her core, and Alice slowly licked her lips, thirsty for another taste of the girl. She just looked so divine, like a feast spread out for her to devour.

"Mrs Martin…" Rebecca whispered, her voice shaky as Alice mounted the bed, planting both hands on either side of her shoulders, caging her with her body. "What're you-"

"Shut up," Alice commanded, the order firm despite the softness of her voice as she leant down, brushing the tip of her nose over the girl's. "Open that pretty little mouth without permission again, and I might just gag you up. Understand?"

Rebecca nodded, her eyes so big and wide as she bobbed her head up and down.

"Good, now stay right where you are…" Alice purred, dipping her head to slide her mouth over the girl's in a ghost of a kiss before sweeping her tongue across her soft pink lips. Immediately they parted in an instinctual plea for more as, despite the warning, she arched up to deepen the kiss.

Alice was faster, however. Greedy to taste more, she pivoted, dragging her tongue down the column of her throat before peppering hot, opened-mouthed kisses over the tops of her breasts. "Mmm… such beautiful tits…"

"Ah… Mrs Martin…" Rebecca panted, rolling her head from side to side as Alice's tongue circled her nipple in a tease at the things she had in store for her.

"You like that? Want more?" Alice purred, keeping her voice low so each syllable would tingle through the tender flesh.

God, it would have been so easy to go down on her right there. To throw caution to the wind and do everything she'd thought about doing to this little tease. To live out all her dirty, little, private fantasies. All it would have needed was just that one little push.

"Yes… yes… I want it… want more…" The words came out in a hot mess as Alice took the pebbled flesh between her lips and sucked. "But why… I mean… oh fuck… you don't seem very… or shouldn't you be more… mmm… mad at me?"

"Oh honey, I'm not mad. I'm furious," Alice promised, her eyes bright with a predatory gleam as she watched her twist and writhe under her sensuous assault. There was nothing sexier than watching a lover come undone. "How dare he keep you from me." She pulled away with a slow draw, lingering just long enough to graze her teeth along her assaulted nipple. Rebecca hissed with the light sting of pain, but Alice soothed it with a swirl of her tongue before switching to its twin. "Mmm... Just look at you. So sexy. You're perfect... my husband's perfect little toy." It was impossible to keep the edge from her voice at that. Just the idea gnawed at her like a dog with a bone, fuelling the blaze in her core. "Well, not anymore. You're my toy tonight."

"Yes... please... do whatever you want to me," Rebecca entreated, her voice rising in a sensuous moan as Alice worshipped that nipple the way she had the first. She couldn't help herself. The girl was just so sweet and lush, a feast spread out to be devoured. Nothing, not even the dirtiest and kinkiest of all her wildest fantasies, could compare to reality. Eager to begin, she pressed a hand between Rebecca's thighs, cupping her mound and sliding two fingers into her drenched heat.

"Oh, your pussy's so wet for me, you dirty girl," Alice said, abandoning her breasts to take her mouth, swallowing the long moan that flowed as sweet as honey as she swirled her digits through her cream. Once they were liberally coated, she pulled back and raised them up so they could both see they were slick and shiny. "I'm going to make you my obedient little fuck toy, but first, I want to see if your pussy's as sweet as your perfect tits."

Eyes locked with Rebecca's, she gave her forefinger a slow seductive lick before putting it in her mouth and sucking it clean, moaning at the musky flavour. "Mmm… you're delicious," she purred, then offered the other finger to the girl. "Wanna taste?"

For a moment, she looked like she might try to refuse, but when Alice pressed the glistening tip of her finger to her lips, they opened obediently. Her tongue slid out to swirl around the digit, licking up the juices coating it before taking it into her mouth, sucking greedily.

"Yeah… that's it, suck it clean, taste your sweet little pussy," Alice ordered. The sight and sounds of the minx's mouth sucking her own slickness from her fingers getting her wetter by the second.

Had she sucked Richard's cock this way? Strangely, the thought didn't inflame her ire, but made the throbbing of her clit so intense, it took most of her willpower to resist the urge to rub it right there and then. So hot and greedy, she was probably a good little cock sucker.

When Rebecca released her finger, sucked clean, Alice smirked down at her. "So, did you like your first taste of pussy?"

With her body almost quivering with need, the girl nodded but looked away from the older woman's knowing gaze.

"Do you want more?" Alice pressed, bending down to trail her tongue down that long neck before pulling back to blow softly over her nipples, stiff and begging for more attention.

Rebecca nodded again, biting her lip as shame and lust tinted her face an adorable pink.

"I can't hear you," Teasing, she dropped her hand to the girl's trembling inner thigh, close enough to feel the heat radiating from her cunt, the skin deliciously smooth and soft. Slowly, she reached a finger out to circle her clit.

"Yes!" Rebecca gasped, so mad with the need for release, the words came spilling out in a hot rush. "More... please... fuck me, Mrs Martin!"

Alice was happy to oblige.

"Mmmm... good girl..." she praised, sliding down her body and laying hot, open-mouthed kisses down her midriff and navel as she went. "You're so sexy... so perfect... my perfect little fuck toy..." With that final claim, she buried her face between Rebecca's legs, dragging her tongue along her folds from the base up to the clit.

"Oh! Oh fuck... Mrs- Mrs Martin...." Rebecca gasped, her head rolling back and body curling up into Alice's mouth as she licked up and down with long, lazy strokes. The flat of her tongue spreading her folds while the tip dipped in to slide through her tender tissues.

All the while she watched, peering up at the girl from between the V-junction of her legs, delighted in the sight of her arching under her mouth, writhing, head thrashing and eyes squeezed tight against the pleasure while her breasts rose and fell with ragged breaths.

"Does that feel good?" she asked, sliding up to circle her clit.

"Yes! Oh god, feels so good!" the girl choked out, completely overwhelmed and white knuckling the tangled bedspread in an effort to grind her hips against her tormentor's tongue.

It was one of the sexiest sights Alice had ever seen.

"You like me licking your pretty little pussy?"

"Yes!" she gasped, shaking with her need.

"Good," Alice purred, giving the girl's clit a sensuous kiss. The musky scent of her flowing desire curled up her nose, as addictive and intoxicating as spiced wine.

"Now whose pussy is this?" To emphasise her question, she plunged her tongue between her folds, licking every part of the slick honeypot she could reach. Heady cream poured past her lips as her tongue probed, twisted, and flicked.

"Oh fuck! It's yours! That's your pussy, Mrs Martin!" Fuck, it sounded so hot when she called her name like that.

"That's right. My husband was only renting it when he fucked it, but you belong to me now," she growled, pushing the girl's legs back towards her chest, opening her completely. Then, curling her arms around her thighs, she dragged her cunt to her mouth.

"Yes… Yes… it belongs to you… oh fuck!" The moans left her in a rush as Alice focused all her attention on her clit.

"Yes, that's it, your such a good girl, such a good little fuck toy… Mmm… you're so wet and taste so good… does my good little fuck toy want me to make her cum?" she asked, shaking her head from side to side so her tongue wouldn't lose contact with the little bundle of nerves.

"Oh fuck! Yes!" she gasped, her tone rising higher and higher while the muscles of her thighs tensed in Alice's hands, her restraining hold just managing to keep her pinned beneath her mouth. "Please… please, Mrs Martin… lick me… fuck me… I want to cum… I want to cum for you…"

"Then do it, you dirty girl, cum for me… cum in my mouth like the dirty girl you are," she ordered, before taking her clit between her lips, her cheeks hollowing as she sucked, hard.

"Oh-oh my god…" Rebecca sobbed, her spine curling at the delicious suction as her hands grabbed for Alice's head, fisting her hair. "Oh fuck… there… right there…. Fuck! Yes! Yes! Ye…" Her words trailed away as her orgasm hit, crashing over her like a tsunami. It didn't matter. Alice took everything she had to give, sucking her through the rolling waves as her hips curled and undulated, fucking her mouth in all the ways that made her own neglected pussy throb.

Especially when combined with the sheer eroticism of watching this beautiful creature cum. Of knowing she'd been the one to reduce her to such a state of base pleasure.

When the storm finally passed, Rebecca tumbled back down to earth and collapsed into the sheets in a quaking mess with a heaving bosom, glazed eyes and flushed checks of a woman well fucked. With a last cleaning lick, Alice disentangled herself. Shrugging off the hand that had been tugging at her hair, she crawled up her body to press an opened mouth kiss to her lips to feed her the last of her own sweetness. Even in her haze, the girl drank it greedily, sucking at the slickness from her tongue with a soft purring moan.

"So, how was it?" she asked, a knowing smirk pulling at the side of her lips as she pulled away.

Rebecca exhaled, her breathing ragged as she tried to gather her wits. "Amazing, Mrs Martin…" She pushed a hand through her bangs, brushing back the tangled tumbles of her hair that had stuck to her misted brow. "Oh god… my clit's still pounding, I can't feel my pussy…"

"Aw? You poor thing. Well, guess that means I eat pussy better than my husband then." Alice teased, rearing back to sit on her haunches. Hey eyes sliding down, the vision of the girl spread out beneath her, spent and ravaged and so beautifully fuckable.

"Well… I don't know if I'd go quite that far."
Her eyes glanced away, her blush deepening, if that
was at all possible.

The mock challenge sent a thrill straight to
Alice's core that made her drenched cunt pulse.

"Oh really, you little minx? I guess that's it
then, isn't it? I was going to go easy on you, but now I
have to remind you of your place." She undid the belt
of her robe and gave a shrug so it pooled around her
feet, leaving her just in the gown. It took all her
restraint not to rip that over her head, too. The cool
night air felt delicious against her overheated skin.

Rebecca's mouth fell open. "Wow… Mrs
Martin, you're beautiful."

"Mmm… flattery won't save you now,
honey." She teased, another spike of pleasure searing
out from her clit at the hungry look in the girl's eyes.
It was nothing short of burning desire. "And what
about my tits?"

"Your tits?" The words were tentative but she
couldn't help staring as Alice leant forward just
enough to emphasise the tops of her breasts, shown
off perfectly by the deep cut of the silk and lace.

"Yes. Do you like them too?" she asked
silkily, lowering a hand to cradle the back of the girl's
head, raising her up. "Do you want to taste them?
Suck on them?"

Rebecca's tongue licked across her bottom lip.
"Yes. They're amazing, but I don't-"

Her words were smothered to silence when Alice pressed her face into her breasts. For all her outward nervousness, Rebecca didn't hesitate and applied lip service to every bit of skin she could reach, peppering the tops of her breasts with fervent kisses.

"Mmm... good girl, that feels... So good... yeah, worship my tits," Alice panted. It was a delicious sensation. The feeling of the mouth on her skin merging with the desperate heat burning inside her and sending tongues of tingling fire flicking over her skin, driving her wild. Fisting the girl's silky hair, she pressed her face hard to her breast, dragging her where she wanted with one hand while pushing the gown's spaghetti straps down with the other, freeing her breasts.

Rebecca didn't miss a beat and dragged her tongue over the dusky nipple, making Alice gasp and arch. Her head fell back with a pleading whimper for more as the girl's hands came up to cup and squeeze her cleavage, sending waves of ecstasy down to her core. Meanwhile, Rebecca's tongue rolled around and around her nipple, winding her up tighter and tighter, before switching to curl and flick over the other.

"Oh fuck, that's it... mmm... yes, suck my tits, show me what a good little fuck toy you are!" Alice moaned in a shuddering breath, the sight of that pink tongue sweeping over her breast working her into a frenzy. Her breasts, though always sensitive, suddenly seemed to be intensely so. The feeling was divine yet woefully inadequate and made her feel ready to burst. Then soft lips closed over her right nipple in a hard suck, and something inside her snapped. Unable to wait anymore, she dragged Rebecca's mouth from her breast and pushed her back down on the bed. She landed with a cute little gasp that was quickly silenced when Alice climbed up her body and sat on her face.

Later, the despicable part of her brain that deals with second thoughts and regret will try to convince her that this was a bad idea. That Rebecca was a girl-sex virgin and she should have found a better way of coaxing her through going down on a woman than just shoving her cunt on her face.

But at that moment, Alice didn't care.

She was desperate, near mindless with the need to cum, and the first stroke of her lover's velvety tongue was like a burst of white hot firecrackers behind her eyes.

"Oh fuck, yeah, that's it, lick my pussy... Yes! Yes!" she moaned, throwing her hands out against the nearest wall to steady herself. Her back bowed with the sensations radiating from her core as Rebecca's tongue went to work, sliding through her folds with long lapping licks that turned her legs to jelly. Turned on as she was, she knew she wouldn't last long.

Rebecca was a quick learner. While her first lick had been a shallow test, nervous and unimaginative, they quickly turned long and smooth.

Then her hands were around her hips, hands grabbing and squeezing her ass, drawing Alice's cunt to her mouth as her tongue plunged deep, drinking her in like she was parched and dying of thirst.

No doubt about it, the girl was a natural pussy eater.

"Oh god honey, you've no idea how long I've wanted to see you like this…" Alice moaned. Just seeing her beneath her, those wide eyes staring up at her from between her thighs as she ate her was stoking the fire in her belly, her nerves from her clit to her nipples were on fire, the heat radiating out to her fingers and toes. "Mmm… your pretty little face between my legs… licking my cunt like the dirty girl you are… such a dirty… dirty gi- oh fuck, oh fuck!"

Whether on purpose or by chance, Rebecca had found her clit, and the feeling of her lapping at the bundle of nerves drove Alice wild. It all felt so fucking good. The tight tingling of her nipples. The throbbing knot at her centre. All The things she was doing with her mouth, that made it feel like her lips and tongue were everywhere, licking, kissing and sucking her all at once. It all came together, and she was about to burst.

"Yes! Yes… Oh god… that's it… suck my clit… make me cum on your face- oh fuck, oh fuck, oh fuck, oh fuck!"

Doubling over, she clawed at the wall for whatever purchase she could find as her hips curled and rocked, grinding her sex into the girl's mouth, riding her face as her release exploded through her. Rolling curtains of an aurora blazed across her eyes as her orgasm crashed over her in great white-capped waves, washing her away from her body into a sea of bliss.

She wasn't sure how long she floated there, but when she finally opened her eyes, never having actually realised she'd shut them, Richard was standing over her.

Chapter Six

Taking in the sight that greeted him on the bed, *their* bed, Richard didn't know what to say.

It was a new experience for him.

Good or bad, he usually could always be relied upon to spit out some sort of asinine observation. Of course, it wasn't every day you walked in on your wife riding another woman's face to what could only be described as an earth-shattering orgasm.

Especially when it happened to just be their babysitter's face she was riding.

The same babysitter who'd been under his desk sucking his cock that very morning.

Ironic, considering they didn't even like sharing cutlery at dinner.

"Well, when you said you had a surprise for me, I wasn't expecting this." He forced himself to speak, the words catching in his throat, as thick and sticky as toffee as the sight of them tore at him. Tore and slashed with icy talons set aflame. The blaze scorched the surface to black blisters while the icy edge cut deeper than bone. It left him numb to the world but merged with the guilt of his own misdeeds to plague his conscience. "You've surpassed yourself this time."

His voice's flat tone and that detached look shimmering in his dark eyes quickly hit Alice in a cold cascade that twisted her stomach into knots of dread. She had never seen her husband look so... She couldn't put a name to it. It was neither anger nor sadness, but something in between. Something that seemed to hone the sharp lines and smooth planes of his broad, handsome face, somehow making him even more devastatingly attractive. Lost, no, forlorn, that was it. She had never seen him look as forlorn as he did just then.

It tore at her heart to see him so wounded, and it hung a weight of guilt and regret about her neck. Whatever her reasons had been, she'd never wanted to hurt him.

However much Rebecca's confession had stung her, the betrayal was only an idea, while he was seeing her with his own eyes. Just the idea of being in his shoes, of walking in without warning to find him going balls deep in the girl's tight little cunt, was enough to make her feel sick.

He was taking it in his stride though and, for all her wanting to comfort her husband and tell him how much she loved him, she saw his challenge. Saw it and accepted it, refusing to falter under his cool glare, but met it head on. Her eyes were hard and challenging even as she gave him her best sexy, faux-innocent pout. "Surprise, *Dick*," she purred sweetly, bending a hand down to stroke Rebecca's hair. "Someone let slip about how you helped her the other night, and well, I decided she needed a little lesson in manners."

And not to fuck with other people's husbands.

"Really?" If he hadn't just walked in on it, it would have been almost impossible to tell she'd just come down from a hard orgasm. Her voice was just as sensuously throaty as he'd ever heard it. His eyes glanced down to where the top of the girl's head was peeking out from between his wife's thighs. She'd stopped what she was doing when he'd spoken, and her doe eyes stared up at him, wide and unsure. "Funny sort of lesson."

"You know me," Alice shrugged, pushing the locks of her dark hair that had tumbled across her face back into place. It was an offhand remark, but he didn't miss the hidden meaning behind the words.

Oh yes, he knew her. Alice was a vixen. Beautiful, strong willed, determined. A woman who knew what she wanted. She also loved her games and could be a right ball breaker.

Hell hath no fury, as they say, and Alice was definitely not a woman to scorn.

"Umm… Mr Martin, I'm er…" Rebecca spoke up, her voice shaky.

"Oh, I think you can call him by his name now, dear. I'd say we're all well past the formality stage by now," Alice cut in, only half teasing as she touched a hand to her hair and, without breaking eye contact with her husband, directed the girl's mouth back to her pussy. "And I didn't give you permission to stop."

They were going to continue with him still there, standing over them. It was like she'd slapped his face.

"Well, would you like me to leave so you can finish your lesson?" Richard asked, trying desperately to keep his voice easy despite the storm of tension gathering around them.

If she sent him away now, then it would be over. Them. Their marriage. Their family. Everything.

Alice held his gaze for a moment, considering. Time seemed to hold its breath, then a current suddenly ran through her and her head fell back with a long moan. "Go? Oh no, no, no, you silly boy, I'm only… only just getting started. Now it's time for you to get your lesson." With her hips gyrating, curling and grinding into Rebecca's mouth as the girl resumed tonguing her clit. She pointed towards the chair that sat in the room's corner. "Go. Si-sit over there- oh fuck, Mmm… I want you to watch. Watch your little slut make me cum again."

And without a word, Richard did exactly that.

It was odd. A part of him knew he should be and indeed was fucking furious. Furious at Rebecca. At Alice. At them both for what they'd done and what they were doing. However, there was another part, a much larger part, the part that had been winding itself up in guilt-ridden knots, that felt almost… relieved. He'd fucked up, he'd cheated, but now so had she.

People liked to say two wrongs don't make a right… and in an ideal world, they wouldn't, but the world wasn't a perfect place. Morally corrupt or not, revenge felt good.

So if this was what his wife wanted to do, to make herself feel better about the situation, who was he to stand in her way?

And after his own misadventures that day, with both Scarlet and Rebecca, it was a much more merciful punishment than he deserved.

Alice could have cried for joy at that moment.

She'd been so afraid. So terrified he might walk out of the room, and her life with it. The relief she felt, watching him drop into the armchair, mingled with the feel of the slick tongue fluttering over her oversensitive clit, almost made her cum again. No matter what, she loved her husband, and always would. She wasn't ready to lose him, but that didn't mean she wouldn't punish him when he'd been so naughty.

And he'd been a very naughty boy.

"Oh fuck! Yeah… that's it, slut, just like… oh fuck, oh fuck!" she moaned, the words leaving her in a rush, her hips curling, fucking Rebecca's hot little mouth as that wicked tongue fucked her. The knowledge that Richard was watching her do this turned her on more than she would have imagined. The throbbing in her clit and the waves of pleasure rushing through felt so much more intense this time round. It all felt so good. So good, her eyes instinctively closed against the sensation, but when she opened them again, it was to see her husband watching her from the chair.

And as their eyes met, it took everything Richard had to stay where he was.

Punishment be damned. His wife was trying to kill him, he was sure of it.

His cock definitely agreed. Despite its vigorous workout with Scarlet, the sight of his wife riding Rebecca's face had roused the organ to new life. It strained against its confines, forming a bulge in his crotch that ached for attention. Called out to be touched. Practically begged to be unleashed and plunged balls deep into either of their sweet creamy cunts.

It was a call impossible to ignore, and he'd almost had the button of his trousers undone when Alice noticed.

"No, *Dick*, oh fuck! No, don't you dare…" she warned in a sweet song of pleasure as, all her lingering inhibitions gone, Rebecca ate her eagerly. The pink of the girl's tongue was just visible between her thighs, sliding through Alice's folds before she switched to sucking at her clit. "Oh! Oh my god… This… this is a punishment, remember. Keep your hands at your side, and just watch. Watch your little toy eating your wife? She's all mine now. You can't touch her till I say, is that clear? Just sit there and watch me cum all over this little slut's face."

Oh yes, they were both definitely trying to kill him.

"Fuck… your such a tease," he groaned, stunned and barely able to believe his eyes, or his restraint. His mouth watered as he watched and remembered the succulent taste of his wife's creamy pussy and longed to be the one between her thighs, feasting on her cunt.

This was Alice he was watching, after all. His wife. His reserved but not at all repressed, little firecracker of a wife, riding the face of their babysitter and obviously loving it. How had he never known she was into girls? Fuck, just the thought of it drove him wild. Now his cock was so hard, it was really starting to hurt. The solid weight of it pushed against his trousers, so insistent it might very well rip through the fabric.

"Oh no, Dick… this isn't teasing. This is just the beginning- oh God, yes, yes, just like that, you naught, dirty girl. Oh God, just like that, that's perfect, that's- oh God, oh fuck, don't stop, I want to cum all over that pretty fucking face- oh shit! Yes! I'm cumming, I'm cumming!" She threw her head back, her eyes closed against the orgasm that seized her, thrashing and bucking with the waves of sensation sweeping through her while her features were consumed by that tranquil, almost far away look Richard knew all too well.

The orgasm seemed to go on and on in one long continuous wave, but was actually a series of smaller intense ones that crashed over just as the last was fading away. When it all became too much and her body crumpled, collapsing to the sheets on her hands and knees, her hips bucking against the girl's mouth. Yet with the girl's arms coiled around her thighs, even then she couldn't escape and she had to push the girl's mouth away.

It was the sexiest thing Richard had ever seen.

As outwardly sensual as his wife was, she looked almost angelic when she came. Watching her cum had always been one of his favourite parts of their sexlife. Yet watching her do so for someone else was like seeing it for the first time, and it was just as exciting.

"Mmmm… you greedy girl" Alice purred, blinking through the black spots fogging her vision and crawling back around to kneel beside Rebecca.

"I'm sorry, but Mrs Martin, your pussy tastes so good," Rebecca explained with a smile that was sweet and innocent despite the wetness that glistened on and around her lips.

Alice made a face of mock astonishment. "Oh, you naughty girl, I'm going to have to punish you for that." Lowering her head, she pressed her lips to Rebecca's in a slow kiss, deep and sensual, drinking her in with lush licks while reaching down her body to the heat pulsing between her legs.

"Mmm… please do."

"I bet you can't wait for it, can you?" Alice softly stroked a finger through her swollen folds before pushing it inside, all the way to the knuckle. Rebecca gasped at the stimulation, her body squeezing Alice's digit tightly.

Alice loved her responsiveness. "Want me to use this pussy again, you dirty girl? Such a tight, naughty little pussy. How did my husband ever fit his big dick in there?"

"I can take a lot more than you think." Rebecca got out. She was trying to sound confident, but Alice could feel the tension amassing inside her, betraying her closeness.

"Well, I guess we better see about that," she teased, withdrawing her finger and coolly looking across the room to where Richard sat.

"Come here, *Dick*."

Chapter Seven

  The low purr of his wife's summons sent a delicious shiver of pleasure rippling straight down to Richard's cock. Dutifully, he pushed up from the chair and, doing his best to ignore his aching cock, walked to the bed, his legs unsure if they were stiff or shaky. Rebecca and Alice watched his every move, their eyes dark and hungry, their lush bodies entwined and ready to pounce like a pair of tigresses watching a clueless monkey walk into their trap.

"That's it..." Alice cooed, trailing a finger through Rebecca's folds, coating the digit in her cream, then raising it up to her mouth to suck it clean with a moan. "Mmm... you've been such a naughty boy, *Dick*. Keeping this tasty little pussy all to yourself. So now you're going to do the right thing and show me everything you two did behind my back."

"Everything?" He asked, his mouth dry as his thoughts swam with the idea of what she was proposing.

"Everything…" The slow curl of Alice's lips was pure wickedness. "I want to see you eat her creamy cunt… go balls deep and fuck her until she screams." Then she turned to Rebecca and, touching her glistening fingers to her chin, guided her to look her way. Holding her eyes, she purred, "and watch you wrap that sexy mouth around his big dick and suck him dry."

Rebecca blinked at the command. Scared and uncertain, she looked like she might refuse before all the desire that had gathered within her won out and she nodded.

"Good girl," Alice breathed, pressing a soft, almost chaste kiss to her mouth, but Richard didn't miss her lips parting ever so slightly. His wife moaned, a sound that doubled the ache in his imprisoned cock as she licked the last taste of herself from those soft lips. Rebecca moaned, her mouth opening under that gentle coaxing to suck greedily at the older woman's tongue as she took her hand and placed it on the bulge of his cock along his trouser leg. Together, they rubbed with fingers entwined, palms twisting and stroking up and down through the coarse material until someone snagged the clasp of his fly tail. They dragged it down while the other dealt with the button.

When it popped free and the vice around his cock eased, Richard couldn't help a sigh. It promptly became a groan, however, the moment his wife dragged the elastic of his boxers back and lodged them a little less than gently beneath his balls. Yet that sting was nothing compared to the feeling of long graceful fingers wrapping around him.

"Mmm... now put your mouth on his big cock..." Alice purred, pulling back just enough to watch, and angled the hard length of Richard's dick downward until the head, dark and swollen, hovered just over Rebecca's mouth.

The girl didn't hesitate. Leaning forward, she took his offered cock into her mouth. Her eyes peering up at him from beneath sex tussled hair as her lush pink lips slid over his crown. The lush heat of her mouth engulfing him in a single smooth glide, cheeks hollowing as she sucked.

Fuck.

It didn't matter that he'd cum twice already. If she carried on like this, he wouldn't last long.

"That's it… mmm… get it nice and wet," Alice teased, biting her lips as she watched Rebecca take him in as deep as she could before pulling back, leaving it wet and shiny. When just the wide crest remained, she reversed track, her hands coming up to brace against his thighs, giving her purchase to push her mouth back down, attacking his cock like she'd been starved of it, making up for whatever she lacked in skill with eagerness.

It was something Alice never thought she'd see. Something she never thought she'd want to. A taboo act of betrayal that she should have found repulsive, but instead was pushing all her hot buttons and made her tingling pussy throb.

Alice couldn't understand it. She was a proactive woman, not a voyeur. She didn't stand on side-lines. Where was the fun in just watching other people have sex? The very idea sounded no different from watching porn, without the deniability. Yet as she released her hold on Richard's cock to let Rebecca have her way with him, she wanted to watch.

This was so much more than pornography. Porn was manufactured, soulless, devoid of life and all the things that made sex so fun, little more than bodies going through the motions. Compared to that, this was art. Pure erotic art in the making, all induced to inflame the senses. The sounds of Rebecca's mouth as it slid along his cock, the way her eyes peered up at him with a knowing yet scared and pleading fashion. The way Richard's breathing changed as his hands fisted against the feeling it invoked in him, even as his body started circling, feeding her more of his cock. Even the heady scent of sex rolling from them to fog her brain had her panting. It was pure carnality. A drug she was powerless to resist.

"Suck it, yeah, that's it you dirty little slut, you like it don't you, you love sucking my husband's dick," she pressed, cupping her free hand over the deep throbbing between her legs, fingers massaging the knot of her clit. Not as roughly as she usually liked, but just enough to stoke the storm burning inside her.

Rebecca's eyes flickered back to Alice, almost sparkling with mischief as she pulled her mouth off their lover's cock. "Yes, but it's just so big. Can you show me how to suck it, Mrs Martin?"

"Oh, fuck…" Richard moaned, head spinning as something almost gave way inside him. It couldn't be helped. The vision of her kneeling there in all her naked beauty, a picture of angelic innocence with his cock still wet from her mouth, rising over her face as she said that. Well, it was almost enough to make him cum right there.

"Oh, you want to watch me?" His wife cooed back, all mock sweetness but for the sultry, wicked look that she fixed him with as she did. A look that always spelled trouble. Hot, sexy, fucking trouble.

Rebecca nodded, raising one hand to follow the line of veins that roped his cock. "Yes, please, teach me how to suck your husband's cock, Mrs Martin, please."

Fuck.

Yep, no doubt about it. They were genuinely trying to kill him.

"Alright, you dirty girl," Alice purred, slinking over gracefully to press a feather soft kiss to the girl's lips before gripping his cock. "Mmm… first, go slow and tease him. Just focus on the head, worship it with your mouth and tongue…" To demonstrate, she did just that, bending down to circle her tongue around the flared crest before wrapping her lips around it and sucking greedily. Already so hard and thick, the heated flesh pulsed with each little flutter of her tongue, his desire flowing over her taste buds and straight down to the slick heat throbbing at her core.

"Oh fuck… A-Alice, no… wait… not so…" he moaned, his hands fisting against the urge to grab her hair, the tip of his cock suddenly tingling like it was about to burst.

Alice ignored his entreaty.

"Then lick his dick like it's the biggest, juiciest fucking lollypop you've ever seen." Releasing his tip to turn her head from side to side, dragging her tongue down his cock's flanks and underside to the root, never once losing contact. "Don't forget his balls... take them into your mouth and lick them all over- mmm," she moaned, her hum reverberating around his balls as she opened wide to lodge one against the roof of her mouth, her tongue stroking the underside, sent waves of lust crashing over him. Holding his gaze, she suckled one then the other, cradling them with her tongue and rolling them over and over before releasing both to lick back up his length. "When he's all nice and wet, worship him with your mouth, sucking like you want to get every drop of his cum..."

"Ah fuck..." Richard groaned, almost beyond speech as he watched his wife suck him deep into her mouth. The feeling of warmth flowing over his cock to draw him into a font of liquid heat almost made his knees give way and he couldn't help grabbing at her head, needing more.

"No Dick, no touching," she snarled, slapping his hands away before grabbing him with both hands and swallowing him. With her lips stretched tight around his girth and cheeks hollowed, she slid her mouth up and down, smooth and steady, taking him as deep as she could on every swing. Forgetting everything else. Her every thought and focus was consumed with the taste of his flesh on her tongue. The feeling of his cock moving through her lips and swelling in her mouth. The tortured ecstasy on his face as he watched her and the feel of his body, taut and straining against itself in the race to orgasm.

These were the moments she lived for. To have so much power over one so big and strong, to drive them crazy with lust, it was more than any mere aphrodisiac. It was enough to make her fucking cum.

"Mrs Martin?" The softly spoken question brought her back to reality with a hot spike that went straight to her clit. She glanced up to see Rebecca watching in awe. Her once innocent doe eyes were dark with lust and her lush mouth opened and closed in quick, panting moans as one hand clutched at her breast, roughly tugging and twisting the nipple. The other was nestled between her legs and was working savagely at her clit.

Guess she likes to watch too.

A fresh rush of heat surged down to her core at the thought of the girl masturbating to a show of her sucking off her husband.

Pulling off, Alice smirked up at Rebecca and slowly licked the taste of her husband from her lips. "Mmm… such a big, yummy cock. He's easily big enough for two mouths. It needs two mouths…" She angled his cock towards her. "Come here."

It was an order that could not be disobeyed. Clearly knowing just what was expected, Rebecca swooped down and dragged the flat of her tongue up his shaft. From where Alice still gripped, up to the tip and the older woman's waiting mouth.

"Oh… Jesus… fuck…" Richard bit out, his words a tangled garble of grunts and moans as their mouths came together around him in an opened mouth kiss.

Already fighting his own building orgasm, he knew he should look away. Should close his eyes or cover them or… something. Anything. Anything to block out the sight of their tongues duelling around his tip, licking and lashing in that erotic battle for dominance that made his heart pound, but he couldn't.

The sight of them together, his wife and mistress, working together to drive him out of his mind. It was just so taboo, so erotic, so fucking hot, that he couldn't bear to look away.

Seeing the tormented ecstasy on her husband's face, Alice took pity on him and pushed his cock up into Rebecca's mouth.

"That's it, good girl, now suck my husband's dick like I showed you…" she instructed, releasing her grip on his cock so she could slide her tongue down the side, tracing the veins that bulged along its length. All the while watching as the girl picked up right where she'd left off, mouthing and sucking at his crown like she was trying to suck every drop of cum out of his balls. "Yes, just like that... I love watching you suck his cock, go on, show us what a good little cock sucker you are..." Her encouragement drew a ragged sound from her husband, and she glanced up to see he was still watching them. His eyes locked to the sight of the girl's mouth wrapped around over his cock. "Does that feel good, Dick? Haven't I made her into such a good little cock whore for you?"

"Yes... oh fuck, so good" he growled out, his voice harsh and guttural and despite herself, Alice felt that knot of jealously in her heart winding tighter.

It was the first time she had ever heard her man sound so desperate. So wild and untamed, and despite herself, that small little voice inside didn't like it. Didn't like that it was this girl's mouth bringing it out of him instead of hers. In all their time together, no matter all the little tricks and games she'd played, she'd never been able to break his reserve. She could arouse the animal in him, but it was still a chained beast all the same.

Alice wanted to be the one to do this to him, to arouse such passion, to break his chains and take him over the edge.

And there was only one way she was going to do that.

She didn't give Rebecca any warning. Drawing back, she raised a hand up to the back of Rebecca's head and pushed down firmly, forcing the girl's mouth down onto Richard's cock. She didn't resist, absorbed in the moment, she went with it, swallowing through the initial shock to take him all the way to the root as Alice came up, curled her free arm around his neck and crushed their mouths together in a hungry kiss.

And she knew, in that moment, for him, it was her mouth around his cock, deep throating him.

It was too much.

The intensity of his wife's kiss, along with the feeling of her soft, sensuous body pressed up against his as the lush heat wrapped around his cock sucked it in all the way, finally drove Richard over the edge. His hands fisted in the waves of soft hair, holding Rebecca right where she was as his hips circled up into her mouth, the instinctive urge to thrust and fuck too powerful to deny. Near molten heat surged up through his shaft, but Alice swallowed the incoherent sounds that flowed from him as thick and hot as the cum he was pumping down Rebecca's throat. She swallowed it all greedily, moaning with a sweet purr of satisfaction that coursed straight down to the base of his spine, adding to the waves of ecstasy.

Then the storm passed. With the last ripples of his release rippled through him, it was as if every muscle in his body had turned to jelly. With spots dancing before his eyes, he stumbled, almost losing his balance as his knees gave with that sent him tumbling into the bed's warm embrace. Darkness clawed at the corners of his eyes and with his heart still pounding like a drum, sleep didn't exactly sound like a bad idea.

Alice, however, had no intention of letting him off so easily.

"Oh Dick…" she murmured, throwing one lushly smooth leg across to straddle him. A small smile playing across her lips as she gazed down at him, dark eyes burning with predatory hunger.

"Wow… it's still so hard." Rebecca voiced as she rolled over and almost straight into his cock, still hard and not showing any signing of shrinking. She let out a long admiring breath and the feel of it wafting across his over sensitive glans made him gasp.

She looked up at Alice. Those big doe eyes, once so sweet and innocent, burned with the same dark, lustful fire that met them. Her tongue slowly swept across her lips. "Thank you for sharing your husband's cock with me, Mrs Martin."

The sweet, almost innocent way the girl said the dirty words, like it was for giving her an extra cookie, sent a fresh shiver of arousal through her. "She's such a good girl, isn't she, Dick? So sexy and polite, and such a good little cock sucker..." In truth, Alice couldn't help being rather impressed. Good as she was, Richard was just too big for her to swallow whole, but Rebecca had taken to it like a natural. And she looked so sexy with her husband's cock in her mouth.

"Yes, so good," Richard groaned, his voice low and tortured as memories of Rebecca's mouth gliding along his cock swam before his mind's eye. Recollections that caused his dick to twitch eagerly.

Fucking treacherous bastard!

Alice cooed a sympathetic sound that did not meet the wicked glint in her eyes. "Now you stay right there, honey, there's something you need to see..." she told Rebecca while turning back to the view of her husband stretched out beneath her. The sight of his hard body still covered by his shirt and trousers, though they were open around his most impressive of attributes, made her arch a brow.

Those would have to go. It was time to reaffirm her claim.

"I can't wait to watch you fuck her." She leaned down to nip and lick at his jaw and neck, running her hands down his chest through his shirt, fingering the buttons open as they went. "I know I said I wanted to watch you eat her tasty little pussy next, Dick, but watching her suck your cock got me so hot, I just can't wait. Dick, I need to get fucked, and I want her to watch it. I want her to see us and know that you're mine." When the last button came loose and the shirt fell open above his already splayed trousers to reveal his taut abdomen and well-defined lines she loved to lick. Not exactly a six-pack, but age, with the help of a good diet and a healthy workout routine, had been kind to her husband.

She rolled her hips, stroking her creamy sex with his length. "You're mine, Richard."

"Yes," he hissed, his jaw tight as her fingers curled around him. Her touch was warm, her hand small but strong, and skilful squeezing returned him to full hardness with a groan. "Yours, and you're mine."

The promise in those words sent a rush of relief flooding through her. The dedication that no one would ever come between them, so familiar yet suddenly so new and important, was as true now as the day he'd first promised her. She could see it in his eyes, the look of savage devotion blazing within them as he watched her notch his wide crest against her cleft, coating it in her flowing cream. More acute than ever before. A fierce promise just for her that made her heart flutter, and core throb with an ache to feel him deep inside her.

"I love you-ohh!" The words left her in a rush, her stormy eyes widening with the feeling of his cock pushing inside her as she let her body drop.

Fuck, she never tired of that burn. The feeling of being stretched, filled, split in half.

"Oh Fuck… no… wait…" Richard groaned, hands grabbing for the lush fullness of her bum, trying to stop her as her inner tissues wrapped around him, squeezing and sucking greedily, trying to draw him deeper. His cock, despite all the day's prior orgasms having leached away much of his sense of feeling, was still over sensitive from the one Rebecca's mouth had sucked from him.

However, his wife was in no mood to listen.

Needing to have him, all of him, inside her, Alice pressed on regardless. Her hands moving to his shoulders, pushing against his restraining hold, nails biting into his flesh as inch after delicious inch filled her pussy, still so sensitive and tender from the night's bounty of orgasms.

"Alice…" he bit out through gritted teeth, his words threaded with pained ecstasy, and shutting his eyes against the delicious sensation. His every sense and reason focusing on their union as lush, velvety warmth enveloped him to the hilt, squeezing like a fist.

"No! Don't… don't you dare close your eyes." She breathed through the sensations, needing to see. Nothing thrilled her like watching him, seeing him so on edge. Looking into his eyes, feeling his cock throb and swell inside her, and letting him see what he was doing to her in turn, the wildfire about to consume her as he reached places so deep inside.

The intimacy was so searingly intense, it was as if they were the only two people in existence. Only when he obeyed and their eyes locked did she move.

She started slowly, with small rolls of her hips.

She always needed to start off slow. No matter how turned on or wet she got, he was just so big, and her body loved it.

"Oh! Oh God... oh fuck, yes, Dick, fuck!" Alice panted, almost losing herself in the feeling of his cock invading her. Reaching so deep inside. Touching all the places she'd never known existed before him. She could feel her inner tissues clenching around his thick cock, refusing to let him go as she circled her hips, making her feel every delicious inch of him.

"Oh fuck, Alice, shit, you feel so good. Ride me baby, ride my fucking dick..." he panted, his breathing almost ragged from the feeling of her cunt tightening around him. Her slick inner walls fluttered with a frenzy as Richard let her have her way with him, wanting nothing so much as to watch her, his wife, ride him to her climax.

The sight of his wife above him, riding him. The thick waves of her silky dark main bouncing in a wild, sexy mess. Her skin flushed from pleasure and shiny with misted perspiration he longed to lick. Her eyes blazing down at him, fierce and hungry. She looked so wild and beautiful. A goddess of sex and beauty, riding him triumphantly, glorious and all conquering.

"That's right, that's how you like it, right Dick?" She panted, her orgasm building fast and strong with each circle of her hips and the grind of her clit against the flat of his groin. Her breasts were so heavy and tender, even the silk of her new bra against her nipples was a torturous tease of friction stirring her up into a frenzy. Unable to bear the confinement, she reached behind her, clawed the fastenings until they popped free, then dragged the straps down her arms and hurled it aside. Then, leaning down, flattening her bare breasts against his chest so her stiff nipples dragged over his flesh, she attacked his neck with hungry sucking kisses, drinking in the salt of his skin. "Mmm… Isn't your wife's tight little pussy just the best?"

"Yes, fuck, the best, always the best- oh fuck!" he groaned, teeth gritted and arching his head back. Giving her greedy mouth free rein to lick across his skin, even as it all became too much. He needed to have her, his wife.

He needed to fuck her as much as she did him. Suddenly, his body was moving, churning up into her sultry rhythm. Drawing back as she rose, then thrusting up to meet her as she came back down, meeting her with wet slapping thrusts that had them both curling in ecstasy.

"Oh! Oh my god… oh fuck… yes, that's it, pound that pussy, pound your wife's naughty little pussy…"Alice moaned, her breath hot and ragged on his skin. Her blood boiling with lust, and burning from the urge to fuck, she bit and licked across his shoulder and neck. Up to suck on his earlobe before claiming his mouth to drive her tongue into his warmth, mimicking the motions of his cock thrusting up into the clinging silken warmth as his hands brought her crashing down to meet him.

Fuck, he was so strong when he got like this, so powerful and wild. She loved it. The feeling of every inch of his masculinity piercing her, filling her to the brim. His white knuckled grip on her hips, almost painful but so good, both steadying her and raising her up, then slamming her down. Driving her wild as they went faster and faster until she was almost bouncing on him, clawing at his body, her nails dragging trails of fire across his flesh as each plunge and thrust found all the sweet spots and sent her soaring to new heights.

Overwhelmed, she reared back, her spine curling in a song of pleasure as her release swept over her like a tidal wave. The sensations hit fast and hard, sweeping her into the starry abyss.

"Yeah, cum for me, babe…" he groaned, mesmerised by the vision of her riding him over the edge, the feel of her cunt wrapping around him, refusing to let go even as he kept up his assault with the instinctual drive to join her in release. To come together, but, fuck, it wasn't enough. His cock was rock hard, but even the sight of his wife's perfect tits bouncing with the feeling of her lush pussy clamping down and sucking him deep wasn't enough to take him over the edge. Nowhere near enough.

"Oh god! Fuck! Yes, yes, give me all that dick…. I need it… I love it… I… I…"Alice moaned out, riding her release hard. Her whole body shivering as he fucked her through the waves crashing over her, and streams of stars blasting across her vision. It was one of the most intense orgasms of her life, a carnal nuclear blast, and it would have been so easy for her to give in and let the feelings carry her away. But she couldn't. She wouldn't. Richard hadn't cum yet. She needed to make him cum. Needed to claim his last release and wash all this away.

And that was when she glimpsed Rebecca perched across from them on the other side of their wide queen-size bed. Her eyes wide with their deceptive innocence, even as one hand kneaded a breast, fingers tugging and twisting the nipple, while the other rubbed herself between her legs, circling over her clit.

Their eyes met amidst the orgasmic haze and Alice knew it was time to kick things up a gear. "I want to see you sit on his face, my little slut."

Richard almost couldn't believe his own ears. Fuck, had Alice really just say that?

Just the thought of his wife telling another woman to sit on his face sent a hot thrill down to the base of his spine that at any other time could have made him cum. Then Rebecca was kneeling over him and the question was suddenly academic as she gazed down at him, biting her lower lip. Her eyes uncertain behind the dark fog of lust.

It reminded him of how she had looked spread out beneath him that night in her room, scared but eager. Innocent yet naughty, his sweet temptation. He gave a nod, and releasing his grip on Alice, giving her the freedom to ride his cock, raised his hands up to cup Rebecca's buttocks, steadying her as she swung one lusciously long leg across his shoulders. Then, facing his wife, she slowly lowered her pussy down towards his mouth, flooding his senses with the thick heady musk of her arousal.

"Oh! Oh fuck... Mr Martin!" Rebecca moaned, throwing her head back in a long moan as Richard's lips enveloped her, his checks hollowing as he sucked hard on her clit. Her flavour flowed over his tongue, rich and thick as honey, and just as sweet as he remembered.

"Yeah, you like that, my little slut?" Alice asked, entranced by the sight of his jaw working, his tongue working with the fluttering licks she knew so well. Fuck, when had she become such a voyeur? Just watching him tease the small pearl of the girl's clit got her own bundle of nerves throbbing. Her walls flexing around him, the aftershocks of her previous release still tingling through her as she remembered the feeling of that very tongue dancing across her clit, so it was almost like she was getting fucked and licked all at once.

Just the thought of it almost made her lose her mind. Needing more, she ground and rolled her hips into his, angling her hips just right so his broad crest rubbed against a sweet spot. "Mmm… feels so good, doesn't it? Sitting on my husband's face? His mouth eating your pussy while I ride him…"

"Yes, oh fuck, so… good… oh yes! Right there, right there!" It was only half an answer, clearly too distracted by the lashing of Richard's tongue, but Alice didn't care. She was just so beautiful like that, caught up in the throes of passion. So wild and passionate, a complete contrast to usual bookish innocence. It made her ache to taste her again and cupping the girl's face in her hands, she pulled her in to claim her mouth in a kiss. Thrusting her tongue into her sweetness to feast on her sweetness, drinking her in the way her husband was doing to her cunt.

Denied any sort of visual but hearing and picturing everything, it was all Richard could do to ignore the way his wife slid along his dick, bearing down on him like a silken glove. Rather, he focused all his attention on making Rebecca cum. Greedy to taste her orgasm, he curled his arms around her hips, digging his fingers into her buttocks and crushing her against his mouth and sucking at her clit.

"Oh god!" Rebecca gasped, dragging her mouth from Alice's and throwing her head back.

Needing more, Alice shifted, leaning in to suckle on the girl's neck as she rocked her hips, her next orgasm building hard and fast. "He's got such a good mouth, but his cock's even better…" she purred in her ear, catching the lobe between her teeth and biting playfully. "Such a big fucking dick, so hard and thick, feels so good…"

"Yes. Yes. Yes!" The words were out in such a rush, whether they were in agreement or a vocalisation of her pleasure, it was hard to tell.

Regardless, the result was the same.

"Do you want to feel it, feel his big cock stretch out your tight little hole… fucking you so deep… making you take every fucking inch…" Alice pressed, trailing kisses down the girl's neck.

"Oh god, please…" Rebecca whimpered, arching up into the other woman's touch, clawing Richard's chest for any sort of purchase.

Richard felt how the dirty talk was affecting not just Rebecca, but Alice too, making him groan into the girl's folds as his wife's clamped down on him, her walls squeezing him tight. His body answered without his volition, bucking and screwing his cock up into her luscious pussy.

"Please what, my little slut?" Alice asked, teetering right on the edge but wanting to watch Rebecca cum one more time. Heat rushed over her with the feeling of his cock moving inside her as she watched that sweet face contort so beautifully with pleasure. She bent down and caught a lush nipple between her lips. Sucking once before swirling her tongue around and around, then switching to the other. "Do you want me to let my husband fuck you? Go on, tell me how badly you want to feel his big cock filling up your tight little cu-"

"Yes! Oh fuck, please, please Mrs Martin, please can I fuck your husband… ohhh god… mmm… I can't wait, I need to feel his dick inside me. Please, let me fuck it, I want to fuck your husband's cock, I need it, I… I… oh fuck!"

Richard felt Rebecca's release break as he swirled his tongue around her inner walls, her thighs snapping closed around his head, squeezing so tight he could barely breathe amidst the smooth, warm flesh as she bucked and ground against his tongue. Regardless, he licked her through it, greedily drinking her in, lapping up every drop of her cream, the taste of her gilding his cock to steel.

Alice felt it too, the sudden surge of his arousal swelling inside her as Rebecca's body trembled and shook against hers. And she watched, avidly, needing to see that look in those big eyes one more time. See the pleasure, the releases, the freedom, the complete carnal abandon all billowing together in a perfect storm within those innocent doe eyes.

See it, remember it, and know that *they* had done this to her.

Just the thought of it shattered her mind into shards that cascaded across the heavens with each fresh pulse of white hot pleasure. Consumed by sheer sensation, she claimed Rebecca's lips in a desperate kiss, hugging her close as their bodies quaked together, clinging to her for dear life until the storm passed. Then the world moved, and they were crashing back down to earth, landing with a soft bounce upon the bed.

Richard didn't hesitate. Almost mindless with the need to fuck, to cum, to bury his cock inside them both and brand them both with his seed. One quick twist was all it took to send both of them tumbling off him to the covers. Then he was up, shrugging out of his shirt and kicking off his trousers, before rolling up onto his knees.

Rebecca's soft round bum wiggled enticingly as he came up behind her and, grabbing her waist with both hands, he rolled her over onto her hands and knees and dragged her back towards him. Still slick with his wife's cream, his cock plunged in deep, going all the way to the root with his first thrust.

"Oh my… Oh fuck! Yes, yes!" Rebecca gasped, looking back over her shoulder at him. Her eyes hot and lusty, calling out to him with a lustful passion in an unabashed plea for him to take her, dominate her, fuck her.

With a low growl, he began to move. Pulling back almost enough to slip free, before driving back home so his abdomen slapped against her checks with a wet smack as she pushed back.

"That's a good girl, mmm… take that big dick… that's it, take it, let him in…" Alice purred, her lip caught provocatively between her teeth and eyes smouldering as she watched them rut. Drinking in the sight of him, so big and strong, using her like a little bitch in heat and dominating her so completely as he drove in with a reckless abandon, like she was nothing but a hole to be used for his pleasure. And Rebecca was clearly loving it, her eyes almost rolling in ecstasy. Not that Alice could blame her, knowing how good it felt to have that cock filling her up. That he felt even bigger from behind and could reach even deeper. "Let your little pussy take it. That's a good girl, such a good little slut. Let him have you. Tell him how good it feels… how big and deep my husband's dick is…"

Stretched out as she was, she lay alongside them with her head propped on one hand and one leg bent at an angle for them to glimpse the fingers of the other reaching down between her legs.

Just like that, Richard was right on the edge.

The vision of his wife spreading her legs open further, revealing the slick and swollen state of her well fucked pussy as her fingers circled her clit, almost pushing him almost past his limit. While this wasn't the first time he'd seen her masturbate, he knew he would never tire of watching her. She was such a sexual woman, unceasingly sensual and a complete agent provocateur. He dared the universe to create a more awe-inspiring sight than that of Alice pleasuring herself.

"So-so big… so deep… Oh my god… oh my god… right there, holy shit, Mr Martin, you feel so fucking good!" Rebecca gasped, mewling like a kitten as her hips rocked, greedy for more, her back curling as she pushed back, straining to take him deeper. The waves of untamed hair spilling down over her shoulders and across the bed as she bowed with the pleasure of it. Head down and arse raised, accepting his cock and the pounding it was giving, her moans muffled a bit by the sheets as she buried her head in them, even biting down against high sobs. Hands fisting and twisting and knotting the sheets as he fucked her. Harder. Faster. Needing to feel her cum just one more time.

"Naughty girl, you really wanted my cock, didn't you?" he husked, his voice low and guttural, thick with a primal edge, the beast in him taking over. "Fuck… such a snug little cunt…" he groaned, loving the view of his cock sliding through her folds, smooth as silk, then reappear slick with her cream. The pretty pink of her pussy stretched wide and her butt rippled with each meeting while his balls swung up to slap her clit.

"Yes, yes, fuck, please, please make me cum, make cum all over your- oh shit, fuck, fuck!" Her pleas were raw and desperate, rising high to the heavens and merging with the echoing *slap, slap, slap* of their meeting bodies. With each draw and thrust, fresh proof of her arousal rolled down his thighs.

"That's it, it feels so good having all of his big dick inside you, doesn't it?" Alice coaxed, her eyes lingering on the sight of Rebecca's breasts, full and firm, swaying with the movements of her body. Her fingers quickened, as if she was trying to match their pace, the tense, throbbing heat in her core spreading outward, spiralling through to her fingers and swollen nipples. "Yeah, I know how good it feels, but you mustn't be selfish…" And just to prove her point, she lent up to catch the nipple of one swaying breast between her swollen ruby lips, sucking gently before spinning away and shimmying around until she was sat up with both legs on either side of Rebecca's head "Now, are you going to be a good little slut and eat my pussy while you get fucked by my husb- oh!"

From his angle, Richard could just glimpse over her shoulder to see Rebecca pressing her face between his wife's legs. Though he couldn't quite see what she was doing, the wet sounds of her tongue were more than enough for his imagination to fill in the blanks.

Alice had no such obstacles.

With her heart thumping as the sexual energy sizzled through her blood, she couldn't bear to look away. Even as her head rolled back into the sex rumpled sheets, she was hooked. Captivated by the image of Rebecca's face between her legs, those beautiful eyes staring up at her from beneath a wing of dark hair while that tongue fluttered over her folds.

It was such an erotic view, one that put her right on the edge as she rimmed her hole, drinking her in. "Oh... Oh fuck... Oh my god... yes that's it, right there... oh fuck... look at you... eating my pussy... you're so sexy... so perfect... so fucking go- oh god, oh god, oh god..." Fireworks burst behind her eyes when the girl's mouth suddenly reacquainted itself with her clit. "Yeah, that's it, that's the spot, yes, good girl, you love that yummy pussy, don't you?"

"Oh fuck, yes, Miss Martin... fuck, I love it... so-so good, more... please... give me more..." She whimpered back, her answer smothered against her folds, but thick with desire and rising high as Richard filled her with his cock, pounding her and deep. Yet her eyes always stared up at her, gaze fixed upon her face and lips shiny with her cream as she sucked and licked.

It was all too much, but nowhere near enough, and each little pull of suction had her fisting Rebecca's silky hair and forcing her mouth harder against her cunt. "Fine Slut, you'll have more." Alice panted, her body burning. Her core was hot and throbbing and unbearably slick from the feeling of that tongue swirling around her clit. "Yes, eat that pussy, my little slut, eat my pussy and make cum all over that pretty face."

The pleasure in her voice was a plea Richard knew all to all too well, a desperate instinctual sound, wild and primal. A sound only he had reduced her to.

He couldn't stand it.

With a growl, he started sliding Rebecca back and forth, fucking her cunt onto his cock in time to meet his pounding thrusts. Driving into her harder, deeper, until his broad crest was banging against the gates of her core. Even then, he couldn't get deep enough, the primal beast in him needing to both claim and punish this little minx.

Alice felt the change in him. Felt it in the sudden jarring thrusts that had Rebecca's mouth and tongue grinding over her pussy, and the moans that reverberated around her clit shot through her like white hot electricity, nearly making her cum every time he went balls deep. Then hands were grabbing onto her and crushing her sex to Rebecca's mouth as the suction around her bundle of nerves grew stronger and more desperate, like the girl was trying to suck in air through her pussy.

"Yes! That's it… yeah, so fucking good… yes…" she moaned, her eyes flickering up to his, recognising the look that burned back at her. Saw how good he felt, how close he was. She loved it. She loved watching him lose it and tilting her head back, she fixed him with a look that was pure wickedness. "Fuck her, Dick!" One hand clutching at her breasts, fingers twisting and tugging at the coral tips to ease the ache inside. The other fisted the waves of Rebecca's hair and pressed her face hard to her pussy as the girl's cheeks hollowed with a suction that had her bucking up off the bed. "Fuck her and make her cum! Make her cum all over your cock!"

"Oh fuck, Alice… don't… stop talking like that…" Richard barked, his breath seething through gritted teeth at the feeling of Rebecca's inner tissues squeezing him. Growing tighter with his wife's every word, tight and hot and wonderfully snug, trying to hold him in, refusing to let go. It felt good, too fucking good.

Alice's eyes flash at his outburst, her heart thumping and rolling and twisting a peaked nipple close to the point of sweet agony. "Oh, does my little slut like it when I talk dirty?"

"Oh yeah, she loves it…" And as he said it, punctuating each word with the slap of flesh on flesh, Rebecca moaned helplessly, her body shaking with the orgasm ripping through her.

However, Alice ignored him, her eyes fixed upon the eyes peering up at her from between her legs.

"You like getting fucked like the little bitch in heat you are, don't you?" She pressed, tightening and twisting her hold on her hair while her hips rocked and ground against her tongue, straining up into the lush heat. Her core was tight and throbbing and eager to cum again. "Look at you, eating my pussy while getting fucked. That's my husband's dick inside you, filling up your pussy, my little slut. Yes, suck my clit while you take his big cock. That's right, make me cum on your face while you take my husband's big fucking cock…"

"Do you like watching your husband fuck me, Mrs Martin?" Rebecca asked, raising her head slightly to ever so softly tongue her bundle of nerves with soft flicks. Yet beneath her pleasure flushed face, her eyes were pleading and desperate, needing to hear it. As if deep down, she still harboured doubts.

"Oh sweetie… I love it, watching you take my husband's cock while eating my pussy is so fucking sexy- oh fuck… oh fuck!." Alice's whole body bucked, an orgasm crashing over her when Rebecca's mouth enveloped her, that wicked little tongue thrusting deep to swirl inside her. It was like she was trying to find and lick all her sweet spots at once, sending fresh waves rippling through her, pushing her release on and on, until black dots were dancing before her eyes.

She couldn't bear it. It was too much. She was too sensitive, and with a last gasp, she pushed her head away. "Enough…"

Richard watched his wife succumb to her orgasm with his own not far behind. The sight of it almost pushed him over the edge, yet he wanted more and stubbornly tried to hold it at bay. His eyes rolling back up to the ceiling, trying to focus on something, anything, to distract him. Distract him from the feeling of Rebecca's lush walls, milking him with greedy pulses. From the sight of his wife writhing in such sweet oblivion, and his cock sliding through the swells of the girl's butt, disappearing inside her sweet cunt.

Seeming to know his mind, Alice, with the spots fading but her body still tingling, lurched up to kiss his mouth. "And you Dick…" she husked, kissing like she owned him. Needing him to know he was here, and she was his. Her hands rubbing their way up the tense muscles of his arms and shoulders to fist the rough brush of his hair, crushing his mouth to hers. "Did you enjoy watching our little slut eat me while you fuck her?" A deep, guttural growl rose in him to answer her, sending shivers of desire rushing up her spine. His control slipping, his hips snapped with harder, faster strokes that literally fucked Rebecca down into the bed beneath them. "Doesn't her naughty twenty-year-old cunt feel good wrapped around your big, hard cock?"

"Yes, fuck, shit, so fucking good…!" He groaned, shaking with the tensions threatening to overwhelm him. The heat of her words tingling down his spine to stir the telltale throbbing down in the base of his spine. "Ahh Shit! Fuck… I'm going to cum!"

"No, net yet Dick." She ordered, pulling back just far enough to flick the tip of her tongue teasingly over his nose, but the purpose burning in her eyes steeled him to obey and linger in that hellish purgatory. "Turn her over. Let's finish her together."

Near mad with his need to cum, Richard didn't question her. Without losing his rhythm, he tensed his grip and rolled Rebecca over onto her back. Rebecca squeaked at the sudden twist, but before she asked, Alice threw a leg over her body and leaned down, their bodies fitting together like puzzle pieces sliding into place, her eyes glued to where his cock was gliding through her folds.

"Mmm… that's it baby… Your dick looks so good going in and out of her pussy." Her mouth watering at the sight of the wetness that was coating his cock with each thrust, she leant in and swept her tongue through Rebecca's folds.

Richard couldn't believe his eyes. "Oh, fuck… Alice…"

She didn't answer. Relishing the heady taste of their mixed juices, she twisted her head ever so slightly to slide between their grinding bodies, licking ravenously, greedy for every drop. Unceasing even as beneath her, Rebecca wrapped her arms around her thighs and bent up to attack her clit, sucking with equal hunger. Swollen and so sensitive from too many orgasms so close together, the sudden rush of sensation was so intense, it was almost too much. But she fought on, suddenly needing both her lover and her husband to be there with her.

Richard already was, and certain he might lose his mind at any moment, he went with her. Blindly reaching down to grasp the back of Rebecca's legs, he pushed them back to frame Alice's shoulders, opening her fully and tilting her hips up towards her devouring tongue. The vision of his wife's head between Rebecca's legs, licking her clit as he fucked her, driving him wild. Past the point of no return, he pounded into the girl's lush grasping heat with his last reserves, going so rough, the bed shook, the headboard banging against the wall in a call that screamed hot, passionate sex to any that cared to be listening. He didn't care. He didn't care if the entire building, or everyone in the whole damn city knew what they were doing. All that mattered was them. He and Alice, together till the dawn, and whatever wonders lay beyond as they walked together, side by side and hand in hand, into this new chapter of their lives.

"That's it Dick, hold her legs back like that... mmm... so sexy... such a sexy little pussy... I love watching you fuck her... yeah... fuck that pussy..." Alice moaned, grinding down onto that wonderful mouth. The high rising moans that poured from her every time she watched Richard's cock driving into the root, reverberating around her clit and through her, out across her nerves, until she felt like a string too tightly plucked and about to snap. Her pussy was hot and throbbing, burning with need. She could sense it in Rebecca too, and met her husband's gaze, needing to see, to watch him go over that edge again. Her eyes were hot and daring him to deny her as she rolled Rebecca's clit with her tongue. "She's such a good little slut for us… yes… Now baby… fill her sweet little pussy up, Dick. I want to lick all your cum out of her… cum for me."

It was a command he was powerless to resist.

"Fuck, fuck, fuck!" he grunted as he pounded into the girl for the final time, burying himself to the root, white hot fire burning out from the base of spine. Stars raced across his eyes with each pulse of heat that shot through him and for a moment, it felt like he was caught in a vortex, having his soul sucked out of his body in the most powerful orgasm of his life. Every sensation was so intense, it was agony.

An exquisitely sweet agony, made all the potent by Alice watching him.

Alice loved watching Richard cum. Hearing the ragged sounds as he dragged in breaths. Seeing the pleasure twisting and contorting his usually so calm expression, the wild look in his eyes. Feeling that shudder course through him as he flooded her cunt. There was nothing sexier than seeing her man climax, and knowing it was because of her. Even now, he was cumming, flooding Rebecca's pussy with his seed for her.

She couldn't bear it. Her own climax hit like a storm as Rebecca's orgasmic moans bombarded her clit. Fuelled by its passion, she pushed him back just in time for his cock to slide free and release the last spurt of his cum across her breasts. Before she took him into her mouth, lips stretching across his crown, cheeks hollowing.

"Oh shi... Alice!"

Moaning at the taste of pussy on his flesh, she sucked hard and didn't release his shrinking length until she'd cleaned it of every drop. Yet that wasn't enough to quench her thirst and even before Richard had tumbled back onto the bed, she'd buried her face back down between Rebecca's legs. Caught up in the trailing after glow of so many powerful orgasms much too close together, she could only tremble and moan as Alice lapped at the mingled juices, thrusting her tongue deep.

Only when she'd scooped up as much of her husband's cum as she could reach did she pull away and, turning around, crawled shakily up the girl's body. With the taste of them still on her tongue, she took her face in her hands and softly kissed her trembling lips, feeding her their mingled juices before cupping her cum-splashed breasts and raising them up for the girl clean.

"Good girl." She praised once the job was done, before pulling her close as she let herself finally give into the softness of the bed and the warm soft body beside her. Then the darkness at the edge of her vision consumed her.

Epilogue

"Where's Alex? I'm guessing you didn't do all this with him just down the hall." Richard mused, staring up at the darkened ceiling above. He hadn't needed to look to know Alice was awake. He just sensed it.

She was snuggled against his right side with an arm draped across his chest. On his left, Rebecca was still asleep, with her arms locked securely around his arm and her head on his shoulder. He didn't bother to wonder how they'd ended up like that. From being spiralled casually around the bed to snuggled together beneath the sheets with their heads just managing to fit together all on one pillow. In the grand scheme of things, that seemed rather inconsequentially irrelevant at this point.

His wife didn't look at him, nor even open her eyes as she snuggled closer, her head resting on the place between his shoulder and pectoral, the softness of her breasts pressed against his ribs. "Hmm... No, he's with my parents. I dropped him there this morning before work and said I'd pick him up on my way home in a couple of days."

"Thank god for that." He grinned, chuckling to himself. "Otherwise, by the time he hits puberty, we'd be spending all our money on shrinks."

That made the corner of Alice's mouth curl wryly as her fingers drew circles across her. "Well, don't count it out just yet. Poor boy, who knows what nightmares he might have after a couple of days staying with my parents... But mum's been nagging for some time with him, so I thought why not take advantage and have a little *quality time*."

It was impossible to miss her sultry purr, and the salacious meaning of it sent a hot shiver down his spine, reawakening his cock, though it complained bitterly at the sums. "oh, so um... how did this..." He glanced down at Rebecca, whose face was a mask of innocence and serenity, betraying none of the deeds she'd performed that day that were at such a stark contrast to anything anyone would call innocent.

Though she couldn't see with her eyes still closed, she understood his meaning. "Her dad thought she'd stolen something of his and got rough with her again."

He stiffened at her words, but the tension in him seemed to disturb the girl on his arm as she shifted suddenly. So he forced himself to relax.

"That bastard," He bit out.

There was so much fire and barely restrained venom in his voice that Alice opened her eyes. "Relax, I took care of it," she purred, leaning in to press soft kisses to his throat as the hand on his chest slid down the line of his abdomen.

"Yeah… how bad?" he asked, swallowing as he felt her hand working lowering, and his body responding to it. Her slow sucking kisses quickly smothering one fire with another. The tempting wench…

Edging higher, she took the lobe of his between her teeth and bit hard enough to make him hiss. "Mmm… let's just say he'll think twice before attacking a woman half his size next time."

"He what!" He jerked back suddenly, his head snapping round to fix her with a look that was almost murderous. "Fucking hell, that's it! I'll kill him."

He meant it too. Alice could see the fury in his eyes, the murder. While Richard would never intentionally hurt her, she'd always known he could and would kill for her. Would do whatever it took to protect her and their son. She loved him for it, and at times it was a major turn on to see and feel him cut loose and go all alpha male.

But it wasn't helping now.

"No, you won't. It's done. I handled it, so forget it," she said, moving her hand back to his heaving chest, urging him back down to the bed. Besides them, Rebecca stirred, rolling away from them. That movement seemed to help ease his storm, and he nodded for her to continue. "Anyway, we came in. I ran her a bath. Then we got talking and…"

"Things came out," he offered quickly, voice heavy and eyes dropping low.

Shame twisted his guts into tight knots.

"Yeah, you could say that," she shrugged, trying to look nonchalant about it, but even as she said the words, she had to look away, unable to meet his eyes.

She still felt it still, that hurt, the sting of betrayal, his betrayal.

That he could have hurt her so cut him deeper than any blade. "I'm sorry, I don't know what came over me… it just sort of-"

She nodded. "*Happened*. Yeah, I know."

The coolness in her tone could have cut glass.

"But now you're okay with… everything." It was a stupid as fuck question to ask and he knew it as soon as he said it, but he needed to know. Needed to know if she could move past this.

"Well, I wouldn't exactly say I'm over the moon about you fucking our babysitter behind my back…" She let the words hang there for a moment, and time seemed to hold its breath before she met his eyes once again. "But then again, I'm not exactly in any position to judge, am I? We weren't exactly playing truth or dare and having a pillow fight when you burst in, now, we're we?"

And just like that, all the tension had suddenly vanished as she smiled up at him.

Despite himself, Richard couldn't help but grin back at her. "No, I guess not."

She nodded. "So, it's agreed then. Next time, we discuss things first, then we fuck them."

Her husky promise turned his cock to stone. "Next time?"

"Well, you enjoyed tonight, didn't you?" she asked, climbing atop his waist so the stiff, and still a little sore, head of his cock was notched against her folds. "No one said it has to stop. Where's the fun in having a bi-sexual wife if you can't experiment a bit?"

"Bi, huh? When did that start?" he arched his brow as his hands brushed down her spine to cup her buttocks, loving the feel of their firmness filling his hands. His wife really had the greatest ass, and though they'd never discussed doing anal, he couldn't help wondering if she'd be interested.

"It's new…" she purred, giving a slow roll of her hips that coated him in her quickening cream and teased her clit. "Something I'm thinking about trying. Care to help?"

"Sure, where's the harm in a bit of *experimentation*…" His hands squeezed her arse suggestively, grinding her harder against his shaft, one finger reaching out, wetting itself in her juices then teasing across her puckered anus, pressing just hard enough to make her gasp.

"Oh! You naughty boy! I'll remember you said that…" she teased while pushing back just enough to feel herself opening beneath the tip, but just the tip. "Maybe we should bring a boy to bed next time. I could suck all his cum out while you fuck me. Wouldn't that be fun?"

"Cheeky," he groaned and, pulling back, gave her ass a swat that had her gasping with a mix of surprise and pleasure. "I think I better give you a spanking for that one."

Alice's eyes lit up at the prospect. "Oh, please do-"

"Ummm… Mr & Mrs Martin?" A small voice cut in.

Stilling, they turned to see Rebecca staring back at them from her side of the pillow.

Alice smiled and reached out to stroke her check. "I think you can call us Richard and Alice now, honey."

However, the girl edged away from the touch, her big doe eyes glassy and lip quivering. "Sorry, it's just… Well, I'm sorry I've caused you both so much trouble. You've both been so kind to me, and I… well… Maybe I should go…" With crystal tears rolling down her cheeks, she threw back the sheets and jumped off the bed, the pale skin of her naked body almost seeming to glow in the low light.

Quick as a snake, Richard's hand shot to catch her arm and pulled the sobbing girl back down to the bed. "Hey, hey… shhh… it's alright…. You've never been any trouble for us."

"Yeah, it's all alright," soothed Alice, wrapping her arms around the girl and pulling her into a hug. "You're safe with us, besides I said you could stay with us while you figure out what you want to do, and so stay with us you shall."

Slowly, Rebecca raised her head to look at the couple, her eyes uncertain, as if she was too afraid to believe them. "Really… you don't mind… even after I…"

"Fucked my husband?" Alice shot her husband a sideways look, her tongue sweeping across her lips. "No, I rather enjoyed watching it, if I'm honest." Bending down, she kissed her tears away. "I don't mind sharing him with you, though I'm not sure I'm ready to share you with him yet. Maybe you should convince me…" She kissed her deeply, licking into her mouth, mimicking the same motions she'd used on her pussy until the girl softened and maned beneath her. "The night is still young, and I think it's time I introduce you to a very special friend of mine." She rolled away, onto the other side of the bed, and opened her bedside table drawer. Seeing what she wanted, she grabbed it and rolled back to face the pair with a grin that was pure wickedness.

In her hand, she grasped a XL magic wand rechargeable vibrator.

"This is Antonio."

The End

A note from the Author

Thank you for reading the sweet Temptations Trilogy.
This is the end of the Trilogy but far from the end for
Richard and Alice. Over the years I've given great amounts
of thought to their respective stories and there is so much
more left to tell. They still have secrets waiting to be
discovered. Their enemies will want their revenge, and of
course, there is the Rebecca situation to consider? Can the
three of them make it work, or was this just a Sweet
Temptation?
This is not the end, it's only the beginning of their
adventures.

To learn about my upcoming works and follow their
upcoming adventures, sign up to my newsletter via:
https://www.subscribepage.com/w7y7k2
Subscribers receive a FREE book with every newsletter.

About The Author

L.M. Mountford's goal in life is to be unique, a character who stands out from the crowd that you just can't help remembering with a bemused chuckle.

A born and bred country boy from the southwest of England, he knew from an early age that he wanted to write and spent most of his time writing story ideas or playing Star Wars on his PlayStation.

Not much has changed over the years, though his stories have grown decidedly dirtier, and he swapped the Star Wars for Call of Duty.

Dubbed the Lord of Lust in 2019 and a firm believer that nothing sells like sex and violence, he loves writing about hard and gritty romantic thrillers, loaded with action men, sassy heroines, and a whole lot of dirty, sexy heat.

He also loves meeting and chatting with readers who love his work. You can connect with him on facebook, or subscribe to his newsletter for regular updates.

Learn more about him and follow his journey on Social Media here:
https://linktr.ee/lmmountford

Bibliography

For a complete reading list, visit LMMountford.com/bibliography/

Collections
Deliciously Sinful Liaisons
Sweet Temptations Box Set
Romancing the Tropics
Just a Number
Alpha Men of the Otherworld
Dirty Daddies
Rogue Warrior
Rogue
The Sweet Temptations Series
The Babysitter
The Boss's Daughter
Just Friends Series
Just Once
Broken Heart Series
Broken
Tropical Cocktail Romance
Tequila Sunset
Beneath the Sheets
Confessions of a Trophy Wife
Forbidden Desire
Stand-alone Titles
Uncovered
Serving the Senator
Training Tracey
Reckless
Daddy's Christmas Surprise

Sign up for VIP newsletter below to enjoy free books, new releases,
discounts, ARC opportunities AND receive a FREE steamy read -
LMMountford.com

Also by L.M. Mountford

Age is just a number, and this collection of sinfully steamy age-gap romances will prove it…

The Lord of lust has done it again and in this anything but sweet, four book Box Set, full of forbidden Silver Foxes and sassy Cougars, he proves that age is no boundary to love, or lust.

A collection of hot and orgasmic stories by The Lord of Lust
Do you love hard men, strong women, sizzling chemistry
and erotic scenes that make Fifty Shades of Grey look like
five shades of beige?
Well, here you go...
7 Books, 7 hard and rugged men, 7 sizzling page turners that
will have you devouring every word from start to finish...

Five years ago, I was the DeCampo Familia's most feared enforcer,
then they killed me…
Now I'm in hiding, a dead man walking.
All I had to do was keep my head down, live a quiet, *normal* life.
But normal is a hard thing for a man like me.
I might just have been able to manage it, if trouble hadn't come
looking for me
In the form of a feisty barmaid.
A vixen probably half my age, with long raven hair and a backside that
promised all sorts of trouble.
Hot, sweaty, all night long sorts of trouble.
I should have stayed away, but I was hooked from the moment she
sashayed through the doors of the bar.
And when a few of the patrons started getting rough with her, the old
me was ready to give them a lesson in manners.
However, times have changed. I wasn't in New York anymore and
getting into a bar fight with five guys for her honour wasn't the way to
this girl's heart or into her pants.
Good thing I'm stubborn, because while her attitude might be frosty,
the chemistry between us is hot and I'm not about to let her get away.
So first things first, I need to learn her name.
And just hope my past doesn't catch up with me
and kill me first…

A Tropical Cocktail Boxset
Romance is in the air in this two book Holiday Romance
boxset that is all about sun, sea and sex...
Tequila Sunset
Beneath The Sheets

Alpha Men.of the Otherworld
The battle of the Species is about to rage, and only the true alpha will come out on top in the Lord of Lust hottest new duo boxset that sees vampires and werewolves lock tooth and claw...

THEIR SILENCE COMES AT A PRICE...

UNCOVERED

THE LORD OF LUST
L.M. MOUNTFORD

When Mina returns for her stepbrother's 21st birthday, she thinks her days of lusting after him are over. Caught up in the heat and passion of the moment, she is stunned to find them back in bed together; their feelings clearly far from resolved.

Haunted by her desire, Mina now has another problem... she must head down a path of lust and desire; torn between the dark delights of the handsome bad boy down the street and her adorable stepbrother who has always been there for her. Can she confront the truth she has long tried to bury? How far will she go to save the one she wants, but knows she can never truly have?

DIRTY DADDIES

THE LORD OF LUST

L.M. MOUNTFORD

The Politician. The Billionaire. The Detective. Three hot alpha males. Three steamy older men, younger woman age gap romances.
The Dirty Daddies is a three book boxset from The Lord of Lust, holding three of his hottest older man, younger woman steamy age gap romances.

www.ingramcontent.com/pod-product-compliance
Lightning Source LLC
Chambersburg PA
CBHW022038170626
46808CB00003B/1260